BLOOD ISLAND

TIM WAGGONER

SEVERED PRESS
HOBART TASMANIA

BLOOD ISLAND

Copyright © 2018 by Tim Waggoner

WWW.SEVEREDPRESS.COM

ISBN: 978-1-925840-42-1

PROLOGUE

600 Million Years Ago

The sun's rays are punishingly hot, the air thick and heavy. Small fern-like plants are scattered across the inlet's rocky shore, hardy, stubborn things that have forced their way upward to claim a place in the light. The water that gently laps against the shore is a stagnant soup of salt and decaying vegetable matter. Not the most hospitable of conditions, perhaps, but nevertheless, there is life here beside the little ferns. Tiny amphibious creatures that resemble what will one day be called tadpoles wriggle through the water, nibbling at bits of algae and dead fern, and if they were capable of anything approaching thought, they would consider this to be the best of all possible worlds and think themselves blessed to live in such a paradise.

These ur-tadpoles are not the only form of animal life in the water, though. Floating just below the surface is an irregularly shaped clump of cells colored a dark crimson. This small mass looks like nothing more than a bit of debris drifting in the water, perhaps a fleshy remnant of some creature that was devoured by something larger, stronger, and even hungrier than itself. But this mass is a lifeform unto itself, and despite its small size and unassuming appearance, it is the most sophisticated creature currently existing on the planet. The Mass is capable of independent movement when necessary, but for now it's content to bob in the water patiently and wait.

After a time, one of the ur-tadpoles swims toward the Mass, intending to determine if this strange object is edible. But the instant the ur-tadpole comes in contact with the Mass' substance, a thin pseudopod extrudes from the surface and whips toward the ur-tadpole lightning-fast. The barbed tip of the pseudopod stretches

1

toward the base of the ur-tadpole's tail and pierces the animal's rubbery hide. Once inside the body of its prey, the pseudopod releases a powerful cocktail of chemicals into the ur-tadpole's bloodstream. The animal writhes in agony as those chemicals race through its body, attaching themselves to the creature's primitive nervous system and the microscopic organ that is nowhere near sophisticated enough to be called a brain. Crimson striations cover its body, as if a new network of veins has appeared beneath its skin.

The ur-tadpole grows still then, and the Mass sends a message to it through their connection. This message is a simple but powerful command, and instinctive rather than cognitive, but if it were to be translated into language, the best interpretation would be FIND FOOD.

Still connected to the Mass, the ur-tadpole wriggles off, the pseudopod thinning and lengthening as the distance between it and the Mass increases. The ur-tadpole – which is now not exactly a part of the Mass so much as a mindless slave to it – heads straight for others of its kind clustered around a glob of algae and eating, blissfully unaware that death is coming for them.

The Mass will eat well this day. It will add the ur-tadpoles' substance to its own and grow larger and stronger. It will save several of the ur-tadpoles to serve as Hunters until such time as it can find better – and *bigger* – servants. Life here at the dawn of time is extremely good for the Mass.

And it's only going to get better.

CHAPTER ONE

The Gulf of Mexico, Present Day

"Slow down!"

Nancy Brock gripped the sides of the skiff to steady herself, an action she knew was useless. What good would holding onto the boat do if the goddamned thing flipped over?

"Quit being so nervous. I know what I'm doing."

Phil Briggs sat at the skiff's stern, manning the motor and – despite his attempt to reassure her – Nancy was confident he'd never piloted a boat before in his fucking life. If Inez Perry hadn't been the cheapest of low-budget producers, maybe they could've hired one of the locals to take them around. She supposed they were lucky Inez had given them the go-ahead to rent a boat at all. Otherwise, they would've had to swim out here to get the pictures they needed.

It was mid-October, but here in the Gulf, it was in the low eighties. The wind was blowing a bit cold out here, though, and despite the warm sunshine coming down, Nancy wished she'd brought a light jacket, or at least worn a top with long sleeves. Instead she wore a black T-shirt with the words *Devourer of the Deep* printed on the front in red letters. The E's were designed to look like little sideways jaws with three sharp, curved teeth – dripping blood, of course. When she and Scott had been given the shirts at the Imagitopia Entertainment's offices, she'd been surprised. Inez was a legendary penny-pincher, even in the world of low-budget films where every dollar had to be stretched as far as it could. When they'd been told not to lose or damage the shirts because the one was all they were going to get, she'd thought, *Now that's more like it.*

Phil wore his production T-shirt as well, along with white shorts and sneakers. You weren't supposed to wear white after Labor Day, but that rule didn't count in places like this, where it stayed warm most of the time. Even so, her shorts were blue, as were her flip-flops. Phil was a lean man in his thirties, tan skin taut and shiny from too much sun, his short hair blond with a light dusting of gray at the sides. Most men she knew would've concealed the gray hair by coloring it or maybe shaving their head entirely. But not Phil. She'd once asked him why he didn't color his hair, and he'd shrugged and said, *"It is what it is, you know?"* He'd risen in her estimation after that. Not much, but a little.

Phil was of medium height, and at six two, Nancy practically towered over him, even when they were seated like now. Her head was a mess of frizzy black hair that moved continuously in the wind as if possessed of its own life, as if she were a gorgon who'd lost the ability to turn anyone to stone. Her skin was much paler than Phil's. She'd lived in LA just like him, but she spent most of her time inside working in front of a laptop. A lot of location scouting – at least the initial work – could be done via the Internet. Unfortunately, all of it couldn't be done with a computer, hence their boat ride.

Nancy kept gripping the sides of the skiff as Phil continued to take them further out to sea. She kept her head turned and her gaze focused on the town behind them, and when she thought they were far enough away from the shore, she told Phil to stop. He obediently cut the engine and then used an oar to row the skiff so it was parallel to land. Nancy let out a long sigh of relief that they were no longer moving. Phil scowled at her, but he didn't say anything.

As he brought the boat around, Nancy found herself looking out to sea. She thought she saw something in the water a few dozen yards away, but she wasn't sure what it could be – if it was even there at all. She had an impression of a rough, dark, uneven surface that made her think of a scab, only this scab was *huge*, at least the size of a football field. She shielded her eyes to get a better look at it, but then the skiff came around and brought the shore back into view. She turned her head, trying to get another look at whatever it was, but she could no longer see it.

"Something wrong?" Phil asked.

"No, I guess not." She looked at him and smiled. "Eyes playing tricks on me."

She turned back to gaze upon the town. She had a job to do, and she didn't have time to worry about optical illusions.

Both of them looked at the town for several moments, taking in the view – such as it was. She guessed they were half a mile away from shore, but even at this distance, Bridgewater looked like shit.

She broke the silence first. "Not much to look at, huh?"

"Maybe they can get some footage of a different town for long shots?"

"Maybe."

They'd have to do something. It wasn't as if the production could afford to mask the town's deficiencies with CGI, the way a major production might. Real life, with all its warts, was much more cost-effective.

Bridgewater was a small town on the Central Coast of Texas, and Nancy supposed that in the not-too-distant past, it might've been quaint, the kind of place you'd go to if you wanted a low-key, laidback vacation away from anything that even hinted at city life. But that was before Hurricane Janae hit three years ago. Bridgewater only caught the edge of the storm, but that had been enough to destroy a third of the town. Nancy had seen pictures of Bridgewater from before the hurricane, and even then the town had looked as if its better days were behind it. *Long* behind. But after Janae, Nancy was surprised that anything remained standing.

The buildings were small, one or two stories at the most. The shore was divided into three basic areas: houses for the well-to-do; shops, restaurants, and bars; and houses for middle-class and below. There were gaps between buildings, indicating places where structures had fallen to Janae's winds. A third of the remaining buildings were boarded up and mostly uninhabitable. There was a main dock which didn't look too bad, but she knew that was because the old one had been destroyed by Janae and replaced by this one, which was less than three years old. The town gave off an atmosphere of decay and desolation which definitely did not fit Inez's vision for the film.

"It would be perfect if they were making a ghost story," Phil said.

"Yeah," Nancy agreed.

"Maybe they could rewrite the script to incorporate the town the way it is," Phil said.

Nancy gave him a look.

"Okay, I admit it was a stupid idea."

Devourer of the Deep had been Inez's idea from the start. She'd hired a writer to bring her concept to life and then told Nancy and Phil all about her "vision" before sending them off to Texas.

The whole world's gone crazy over those dinosaurs they found on that island. There's going to be a big-budget studio movie about them – it's already in pre-production – but if we can move fast, we can film our version of the story and get it out before the official version is finished shooting. We won't do exactly *the same story, of course. That would be plagiarizing. Or stealing. Whatever. Our movie is going to be* inspired *by real events. Besides, there have been a billion rip-offs of* Jaws *over the years, and none of them ever got sued . . . as far as I know. Besides, you can't copyright the concept of sharks eating people. Same goes for sea monsters. People are starving for more dino action, and we're going to give it to them. We'll be a hit!*

A "hit" for a studio as small as Imagitopia Entertainment meant going straight to video and Netflix. In other words, being a modest success.

Nancy had to admit that Inez's reasoning was sound enough. The pliosaur attack on the island resort of Elysium had been a worldwide sensation, but aside from some images of a few dead creatures and some amateur video uploaded to the Net, the world hadn't really seen the pliosaurs. Not enough to satisfy their curiosity, at any rate. Nancy had heard that Animal Planet was doing a documentary on the pliosaurs, but she had no idea when it would be shown. So Inez really could beat everyone to the punch with her movie. And if it was crappy, so what? It would be *first*.

The problem with Inez – actually, one of many – was that she could be rigid when it came to her "visions." Elysium had been one of the most luxurious resorts ever created, and so the town in the script was also a resort. Nothing as elaborate as Elysium, of course. Imagitopia didn't have the budget for it. But Inez wanted a "resort-type town," as the script indicated. Before Janae, Bridgewater might've fit the description if you squinted your eyes and let your vision go out of focus. But now? No fucking way.

"What if we film the town from different angles?" she suggested. "Try to avoid shooting the shitty parts."

Phil gazed at the town for several moments, considering.

"That *might* work," he said at last. "They won't be able to shoot from as far out as we are, though. They'll have to be a lot closer if they don't want to get any of the abandoned buildings in the shot."

He was right, of course. Most likely the director wouldn't even bother trying. Nevertheless, Nancy removed her phone from her shorts pocket and began taking pictures of the town. Regardless of what she and Phil recommended, Inez would want to see for herself. Getting decent pictures while the skiff was bobbing on the waves was difficult, but she managed.

So far, she was pleased at how this trip was turning out. At first, she hadn't been thrilled to learn she'd be working with Phil. He was professional and a nice enough guy, she supposed, but he was married and had a reputation for getting handsy with his female co-workers. He hadn't done anything so severe that he'd gotten fired over it, but he'd done more than enough to make her leery about being alone with him, like out here on the ocean in a skiff, far enough from shore that no one would hear her if she screamed.

But Phil had been a perfect gentleman during this trip. From the flight from LA to the drive to Bridgewater, to getting set up in separate rooms in the cramped, mildew-ridden cracker box that served as their hotel, he hadn't given her any reason for concern. No leering looks when he thought she couldn't see, no suggestive comments, no "accidental" physical contact. He'd given her no reason to worry so far, and while she knew better than to let her guard down entirely – she did work in movie business, after all – she didn't need to be on high alert the whole time either.

As she prepared to take a few last photos, she saw something strange on her phone screen. A reddish-gray triangular shape sliced through the water, and her mind instantly supplied a word for it. *Shark.*

She lowered her phone so she could look at the shark fin with her own eyes. She couldn't tell exactly how close the shark was to the skiff or how big the fish was, but it was definitely a shark. She'd never heard of one colored red before. Weird.

She pointed toward the fin. "Check it out."

Phil looked in the direction she indicated. He saw the fin and shrugged.

"So? There are probably lots of sharks around here. They're nothing to worry about." He gave her a smile. "This is real life, not the movies."

She didn't care for his patronizing tone, but she didn't respond. He was right, after all. Sharks were just animals, and so long as she and Phil stayed in the skiff, they'd be fine. But the sight of that fin, with those strange red striations running through its gray hide, still made her nervous. Ever since the news of the pliosaur attack on Elysium came out, she'd been fascinated with the creatures, like so many other people on the planet. But her fascination turned to revulsion when she watched the online videos of pliosaurs killing people. She began imagining what it must have been like for the pliosaurs' victims, to see a monster out of the prehistoric past coming toward them, mouth yawning wide to reveal twin rows of deadly razor-sharp teeth. She'd begun having nightmares where she was swimming in the ocean, no land in sight, when pliosaurs surrounded her and attacked one by one, each taking a bite of her flesh and then swimming off to swallow it while another pliosaur came at her. The nightmares became so intense and so frequent that she'd gone to the doctor for some heavy-duty sleeping pills. The nightmares lessened in frequency after that, although she still had them from time to time.

So when she learned that Inez was hot to make a pliosaur-eating-helpless-victims movie, she wanted nothing to do with it. But then she realized that if she let her fear control her, she'd never be free of it. So when Inez told Nancy that she wanted her to go with Phil and scout Bridgewater as a possible location for *Devourer From the Deep*, she'd said yes.

But now, out here on the water, seeing the shark's fin – even though it wasn't that close – she was reminded once again of the pliosaurs, and how no one really knew what lay beneath the surface of the ocean, knew what sort of things swam in the dark depths, hungry and hunting for fresh meat . . .

Her gaze remained focused on the shark fin when something grabbed her from behind. She squealed in fear and surprise, and it took her a couple of seconds to realize that a shark hadn't lunged out of the water and fastened its jaws around her middle. Instead of teeth, what gripped her were hands – *Phil's* hands – and they had clasped her boobs and were now kneading them none too gently.

For a second, she was so shocked that she didn't react, but then she grabbed his wrists and tore his hands away from her breasts. Still holding onto his wrists, she half turned to face him.

"What the fuck do you think you're doing?" she shouted. She was both angry and afraid, and she hoped the latter emotion didn't show in her voice.

He smiled as he pulled his arms free from her grip. He did so without any apparent effort, and she realized he was stronger than he looked.

"I was just playing around," Phil said. "No hard feelings, okay?"

Her anger grew hotter, eclipsing her fear.

"You grabbed my tits! How the fuck is that just 'playing around'? More like physical assault!"

"C'mon, copping a feel may make me a creep, but it hardly qualifies as assault."

"What about your wife?" she demanded.

Phil shrugged. "She's a makeup artist, and she's on set in Ontario. Besides, we have a don't ask, don't tell policy. She's probably fucking her way through half of Canada. So long as she fucks me when I want, what do I care?"

It required an effort, but she kept her features composed and her tone relatively calm.

"We've seen what we needed to see. Let's head back to shore."

Phil had continued to smile this entire time, but now his smile fell away and his brow knitted. His eyes flashed with anger and his tone was strained as he spoke.

"You don't have to be a bitch about this."

She held his gaze. "Yeah, I do. Now let's go."

"What if I say no?"

"I'll pilot the skiff myself."

"What if I won't let you?"

Her fear began to grow once more, quickly overtaking and surpassing her anger. There was a teasing tone in his voice, but his eyes were utterly without humor. She wasn't a match for him physically, and she didn't know any self-defense techniques. There was nothing she could do to stop him from attacking and raping her if he wanted. And when he was finished, if he didn't want her to talk about what had happened, he could strangle her and throw her overboard as a treat for the red-finned shark. He'd make up some kind of bullshit story about how she'd fallen into the water on her own and vanished beneath the waves. There was a decent chance he'd get away with her murder.

She couldn't stay here. Better to jump into the water and risk the shark.

Part of her wondered if she was letting her fear get the best of her. Just because a guy grabbed your tits didn't mean he wanted to kill you. But she couldn't control her fear any longer. She'd been date raped in high school by her best friend's brother, and being in this situation now, trapped on the water with Phil, was dredging up emotions she'd felt then. Shame, disgust, anger, self-blame, and with them came a new emotion, an overpowering need to protect herself, no matter what.

She stood, the motion making the skiff shimmy alarmingly. Phil grabbed the sides of the boat in an attempt to steady it.

"What the hell are you doing? Do you want to capsize us?"

She ignored him and prepared to dive into the water, but then she caught sight of the shark once more. In the time they'd been arguing, it had drawn nearer to the skiff, and now it was only a few yards away, red-veined fin slicing through the water's surface like a razor. Had the shark been attracted by their yelling? Were sharks lured by sound? She had no idea, and right then it didn't matter why it had approached the skiff. It only mattered that it was there.

She hesitated, reluctant to enter the water with the shark so close. Plus, she was only an adequate swimmer. Now that some of her initial panic was dying down, she wasn't confident she'd be able to make it all the way to shore even if the shark hadn't been there.

Phil looked toward the shark's fin, then he stood and took hold of her shoulders.

"Don't do it! I know what I did was an asshole move, but it's not worth risking your life over. I promise I won't do anything else to freak you out if you just sit –"

The skiff shuddered as it struck something, the impact knocking both Nancy and Phil off balance. Nancy fell into the boat, but Phil pitched over the side, arms waving in a futile attempt to regain his balance and stop his fall. At first Nancy thought the shark had rammed the skiff, but when she didn't hear a splash, she realized Phil hadn't gone into the water. As she pushed herself into a sitting position, she smelled a strong coppery odor that made her think of a pile of old pennies.

She looked in the direction Phil had fallen and saw him lying face up against the uneven dark-red surface of . . . She didn't know exactly what it was. She recognized it as the strange object she'd seen earlier, the one she'd dismissed as an optical illusion.

We must've drifted toward it, she thought. But then another far more disturbing thought came to her. *Or it drifted toward us.* Whatever it was, it was big. Her previous estimate of its size had been conservative. It was more like a football field and a half long, maybe even two fields. She couldn't get a sense of the entire thing from her vantage point in the skiff, but she had the sense it was irregularly shaped but more or less circular. It rose several feet above the water, but it bobbed up and down, causing water to flow over its surface.

Almost as if it's trying to keep itself moist, she thought.

Her initial impression that the object resembled a gigantic scab was reinforced by seeing it up close. And now that she was sitting up and looking directly at it, the coppery smell was overwhelming. There was something about it that made her stomach turn, and she felt hot bile splash the back of her throat.

Phil didn't seem to have been injured by his fall – and part of her was disappointed by this – but he made no move to get up. She was tempted to start the skiff's engine and return to shore, leaving him here, but she couldn't bring herself to do it. He might have been a scumbag, but that didn't mean he deserved to be stranded. The skiff had floated away from the gigantic scab after bumping into it, and Nancy used an oar to bring the boat back to the edge where Phil had fallen.

She reached out her hand.

"Come on. I'll help you get in," she said.

But he didn't move.

Rivulets of sea water washed over him as the island – because that's what it seemed like to her, an island made of a billion scabs – bobbed up and down. He spat out the water that flowed into his mouth and coughed. She then realized that he was struggling, muscles straining, as if something was holding him to the surface of Scab Island and he was desperately trying to break free.

"Are you stuck?"

She felt stupid asking this question, but it was all she could think to say.

"Yeah, it's like this fucking thing is made of glue."

He gritted his teeth and strained again, trying to pull free, but he couldn't budge.

"Maybe if I climbed over there, I could –"

"Don't! You'll just end up getting caught too. See if you can get a signal and call someone. The town sheriff or the fucking Coast Guard. Anyone. Maybe they can –"

He screamed then, so loud and strong that Nancy screamed too out of reflex. His body began bending in the middle, head and feet moving toward each other, and she heard the horrible sound of his spine cracking. She didn't think it was possible for his scream to get any louder, but it did, and then the air was split by a sharp *crack* as his spine broke. He was folded almost in two now, his arms and legs still stuck in the island's scab-like substance which stretched upward as he was pulled downward. And then, with a sudden wet *schlurp* sound, Phil was pulled inside the thing and was gone. The surface reformed to cover the hole left by his passage, and within seconds it was as if nothing had happened.

For several moments, Nancy could only stare at the spot where Phil had disappeared. A thought slowly formed in her mind and forced its way through her shock and disbelief to the forefront of her consciousness.

It's not an island. Whatever it is, it's alive, and it just ate Phil.

This was followed by another thought, one that nearly made her break into hysterical laughter.

I should tell Inez about this. Who needs special effects when there's a real monster to film?

The skiff had begun drifting away from the . . . the Mass once more, and Nancy's mental paralysis broke. All she wanted to do was get away from this fucking thing before it could do to her what it had done to Phil.

She'd never piloted a boat before, but she'd watched Phil do it, and she was highly motivated. She got the engine started and within moments she was racing toward shore. The prow of the skiff slapped the waves as it headed toward land, and she knew she was probably going too fast, but she couldn't make herself slow down. She wanted off the ocean *now*, and once she was back on land, she'd never go out onto the water again. Fuck Inez, fuck Hollywood. She'd move back home to Indiana, find some boring job, and think about going to grad school.

Salt spray washed over her face, making it hard to see. She squinted to keep the stinging water out of her eyes, but it only helped a little. She figured she was about halfway to shore when she saw the shark leap out of the water in front of her. She didn't have time to react, let alone alter the skiff's course, and she could only watch as the shark – completely out of the water now – opened its mouth wide. As the maw of double-rowed serrated teeth came toward her, she saw that the shark's white belly was shot through with crimson veins. More than that, she saw something like an umbilical cord – dark-red and two inches around – was attached to its tail and trailed down into the water.

That's weird, she thought, and then the shark slammed into her, sank its teeth into her shoulders, and bore her body beneath the water as the now empty skiff continued onward.

She didn't see the boat slow because there was no one left to work the throttle, and she didn't see the other shark fins break the surface, more than a dozen, all of them covered with crimson veins.

* * * * *

The Mass absorbed its twin meals with swift efficiency, reducing flesh, organs, and bone to an easily digestible chemical slurry. Small tunnels opened to allow Nancy and Phil's clothing to pass through the Mass' underside, and the not-food was carried away by the ocean current. The Mass could not taste its food, but it felt a sense of satisfaction at being fed. The hunting was good in these waters, so it would remain here, for a time at least, and see what else it could find to eat.

CHAPTER TWO

"Do you really think it's possible that a species of prehistoric monster has somehow survived to the present day?"

"I do."

A man and a woman walked on the beach close to the water's edge. Waves rolled gently into shore and seagulls drifted lazily over the sand, searching for any edible scraps they could find. The man was tall and thin, in his late sixties, with a head of startlingly white hair and a neatly trimmed goatee the same shade. He wore a pair of wireframe glasses behind which lay intense, almost icy blue eyes. It was sunny out, but the man wore a long-sleeved black pullover, a pair of dark blue slacks, and black dress shoes that were ill-suited to walking on sand. The woman was shorter than the man by a foot and a half, and younger by thirty years. Her black hair was short, and she wore a white bikini top and cut-off jeans. Her body was toned and muscular, her breasts large, and the bottoms of her ass cheeks protruded from her shorts. Her feet were bare, and she had no trouble negotiating the sand.

"You must remember that these creatures are not monsters," the man said in a professorial voice. "They are merely animals. Amazing animals, yes, but still part of the natural world. Are they dangerous? Of course, but no more so than any other large predator. So long as we do not venture into the water, we have nothing to fear. In water, they are the masters, but *we* rule the land."

The woman opened her mouth to reply, but before she could speak, a large form burst out of the water near them. It was a huge reptilian beast, with an elongated snout, mouth filled with sharp white teeth, and black eyes gleaming with ravenous hunger. The pliosaur lunged toward the woman, and she raised her hands in a feeble attempt to shield herself and released an ear-splitting shriek. The man reached for her, intending to grab hold of her arm and pull her backward, but as fast as the beast was moving, it appeared he had little chance of saving her.

Then the pliosaur jerked violently and a sound like an explosive blast of flatulence came from somewhere deep inside it.

The man's shoulders slumped and he let out a deep sigh.

"Seriously?"

"Damn it! Cut! *Cut!*"

A stocky man with a shaved head and soul patch on his chin walked briskly toward the man and woman – and the now immobile pliosaur. He wore white shorts, sandals, and a black T-shirt that had the words *Devourer from the Deep* printed across the chest in red letters designed to look like they were dripping blood. He ignored the man and woman and went straight toward the pliosaur which remained statue-still.

"Fuck, fuck, fuck, FUCK!" He turned away from the pliosaur and called out, "Enrique! Get your ass over here! Everyone else, take fifteen. Hell, take a goddamned half hour."

A rail-thin man with a curly black hair came running across the sand toward the pliosaur. He too wore a *Devourer from the Deep* T-shirt. The camera and boom mike operators lowered their equipment and stepped away from the two actors.

Jarrod Drayton – the older man in the black pullover – reached into his pocket for a pack of cigarettes and came up empty. Had he forgotten them? Frowning, he turned to look for his assistant, Tasha, and nearly jumped when he saw the twenty-something girl standing less than a foot away. He hadn't heard her approach; it was as if she'd materialized out of thin air. She held an unlit cigarette in one hand, a lighter in the other.

"Darling, you are a certified treasure," he said, smiling.

Tasha grinned as he took the cigarette. He leaned forward and she lit it for him, and then he leaned back, drew in a double lungful of smoke, and breathed it out through his nostrils in a slow, contented sigh.

"Thank you, love. That was just what I needed."

Tamara Young, who a moment ago had looked terrified at the prospect of being eaten by a prehistoric monster, wrinkled her nose in disgust. She stepped back several feet and crossed her arms over her chest.

"Good thing we're not shooting any kissing scenes today. I don't like making out with guys who taste like ashtrays."

Jarrod – who loathed being called *Jere* – was tempted to blow smoke into her face, but he resisted the juvenile impulse.

One good thing about dying, he thought. *I don't have to worry about lung cancer.*

Tasha flinched as if she'd been struck.

"Are you all right?" Jarrod asked.

She gave him a shaky smile.

"I'm fine. Got a speck of sand or something in my eye, that's all." She rubbed her left eye as if to illustrate her point.

Jarrod might never have been what some would term a serious actor. He'd never been nominated for an Oscar, Emmy, or even a People's Choice Award. He specialized in horror movies, the schlockier the better. But he knew a lousy performance when he saw it. Tasha had lied about her eyes, he was almost certain of it, but he didn't know why.

Tasha Bates was in her early twenties – although she looked like a teenager. She was petite, which added to the impression she was still a child. She had short, straight brown hair, a round face with delicate features, and she was tan from spending so much time in the sun. Like the rest of the crew – such as they were – she wore a *Devourer from the Deep* T-shirt, along with a pair of what he thought were too-short jeans shorts. She was barefoot, which made negotiating the sandy beach easier.

"Anything else you need, Mr. Drayton?" Tasha asked.

"Call me Jarrod." He'd told her this at least a hundred times already during this shoot, but it was the one thing she couldn't seem to bring herself to do. "And no, thank you. Unless I miss my guess, we'll hang around here for a while waiting for our 'Devourer' to be fixed, and when that doesn't happen, Inez will call it a day and dismiss us."

"Fucking cheap-ass practical effects," Tony Jennings muttered. The camera operator, an African-American man in his forties, was a seasoned veteran of a hundred Z-grade motion pictures, and because of this, he wasn't afraid to speak his mind. Jarrod liked this about him very much.

"I like the dinosaur," Nina Ichatri said. "I think it looks cool."

Nina was of Indian descent and about a decade younger than Tony, still young enough not to be jaded. Jarrod found her charming.

Jarrod thought the dinosaur looked about as realistic as Tamara's fake breasts, which was to say not very. He'd seen images of the creatures that had attacked the island of *Las Dagas*. The whole damn world had. They were magnificent animals, kind of like short-tailed crocodiles with flippers instead of legs. Their pliosaur looked like a generic monster: dragon head filled with oversized fangs, beady eyes, rounded back, body covered in black rubber hide. No personality at all. The thing was currently positioned in the water just offshore, where Enrique Stone – the film's special effects man – stood up to his waist in the water, opening a rubber-covered metal panel so he could get a look inside the machine.

"You really think Inez will end early?" Tamara asked.

Jarrod took another drag of his cigarette and nodded.

"I've been making films since the late seventies. I can smell a mini-disaster on a production from a mile away."

Halfway up the beach, Saul was conferring with Boyd Campbell, the screenwriter, and Inez had walked over to join them. Jarrod nodded in their direction.

"How much do you want to wager that Saul and Inez are trying to convince poor Boyd to rewrite some scenes in case Enrique can't get the star of this picture functional any time soon?"

Boyd was in his thirties and looked to Jarrod like the Platonian ideal of a hungry young screenwriter. Tall, thin, unkempt brown hair, mustache and goatee, and black-framed hipster glasses straight out of the 1950's. He looked like a giant next to Inez, who stood a couple inches shorter than five feet. She was in her sixties, had fiery red hair that matched her disposition, and wore too much makeup and jewelry. She had a habit of speaking too loudly, and Jarrod didn't know if this was one of the techniques she used to intimidate people or if she was simply hard of hearing.

Standing off to the side not far from Nina and Tony, were a man and a woman wearing the same costumes as Jarrod and Tamara. Pete and Shari Dawson did double duty on this production. They both had small parts in the film and also did all the stunts. Pete, who was decades younger than Jarrod, looked ridiculous in his wig and fake beard. Shari was closer to Tamara's age, and her wig didn't look too bad. She was more athletically built than Tamara – both Shari and Pete kept themselves in excellent shape – but her natural breasts were far smaller than Tamara's store-bought ones. Jarrod doubted the audience this film was aimed at would notice the difference during the action scenes, and if they did, they'd likely just laugh. Movies like these were always covert comedies as far as Jarrod was concerned.

The crew for *Devourer from the Deep* was so small, it made guerilla filmmaking look bloated and overbudget. *Lean* and *efficient* were the words Inez used to describe how she liked to work. *Cheap* was Jarrod's preferred descriptor, followed by *tacky*. But there was sun on his face, an ocean breeze in his hair, and while he might not be performing Shakespeare, he was still working at the craft he loved. Being here definitely beat sitting in his home in Thousand Oaks feeling depressed and drinking himself into oblivion, so all in all, he couldn't complain. Except for the whole dying thing, that is.

Tamara had removed her phone from wherever on her nearly naked body she'd managed to conceal it and was checking texts and social media. Pete and Shari were talking in intense whispers – probably having another fight, Jarrod thought. Those two were always arguing. Tony looked bored, and Nina just kept smiling, as if she still couldn't believe she was working on a *real* film – and on location, yet!

Adorable, Jarrod thought.

His cigarette was only halfway reduced to ash when Tasha said, "You were right."

Before Jarrod could ask what she meant, Inez, Boyd, and Saul stopped talking and they all looked toward Enrique. The man had both arms inside the mechanical pliosaur up to the elbows, almost as if he were a veterinary surgeon conducting an operation on a very exotic animal.

"Well?" Inez called to him.

Enrique looked at her and shook his head.

"Fuck," Inez muttered. She then turned to address the cast and crew. "That's it for today. Damn it. Be back here at six a.m. sharp, and we'll pick up where we left off." She turned back toward Enrique and raised her voice. "*Exactly* where we left off, yes?"

"Yeah," Enrique muttered without turning to look at her. "Sure thing."

He didn't sound all that sure to Jarrod, though. Evidently, he didn't to Inez, either, for she glared at Enrique. But she didn't say anything more to the man and returned to what was becoming a somewhat heated three-way conversation between herself, Saul, and Gordon.

Jarrod took a last pull on his cigarette, then he removed it from his mouth, bent down, and put it out on the sand. He then put the butt in his pants pocket. He'd toss it in the trash when he got back to his hotel room.

"I'll be in Flotsam later if anyone would like to join me," he announced.

No one responded, but they didn't need to. Jarrod knew they'd all show up at the bar sooner or later. There was nothing else to do in Bridgewater except drink, and Flotsam was the bar closest to the piece of shit hotel where they were all staying.

As cast and crew began trudging up the beach, Jarrod turned to look at Tasha. She was standing at the edge of the water, staring out across the ocean. He walked over to stand next to her. He looked at the water as well, but he didn't see anything special. A couple of watercraft, some seagulls, but that was about it.

"Something bothering you?" Jarrod asked.

He liked Tasha quite a bit. Not in a sexual way, of course. He was old enough to be her grandfather, for god's sake. Besides, he was gay, although as it had been some years since his last serious relationship, he was beginning to think he qualified as asexual these days. He liked Tasha because she exuded a youthful energy he found refreshing, along with a complete absence of the cynicism that seemed to eventually affect everyone in this business. And she had the uncanny ability to anticipate his needs and was ready to take care of them before he could ask. That quality was a bit spooky at times, but it only added to her charm as far as he was concerned.

For a moment, Tasha didn't respond to Jarrod's question, but then she blinked several times and gave her head a small shake, as if to clear it.

"Everything's fine," she said, giving him a smile. "Just thinking."

Jarrod returned the smile and put a hand on her shoulder.

"My dear, if you hope to make any kind of life for yourself in this business, *thinking* is the last thing you should do."

* * * * *

The Mass lay a half mile off shore, submerged to a depth of twenty feet. When the sun grew too warm and the Mass' surface started to dry out, it descended into the ocean to cool itself and rehydrate, which is what it had done now. It rested during these times, for its system – while primitive in many ways – was staggeringly complex, and it needed time to recalibrate the intricate neural network linking its trillions and trillions of cells. The creatures that served as its Hunters could not remain motionless, however. If they ceased swimming, no water would flow through their gills and they would not be able to extract any oxygen from it, and thus they would die. So while the Mass rested, its Hunters – which currently numbered an even three dozen – swam in slow, lazy circles, and unless food was foolish enough to come too close to their jaws during this time, they left it alone.

These Hunters were far more efficient than the first small ones it had taken so very long ago, when it too had been much smaller. They were swift and strong, perfectly designed to hunt and kill in their environment, and they served the Mass well. The Mass had to absorb them and find new ones every few years. Once they joined the Mass, they were unable to procreate, so the Mass couldn't simply breed more servants. But that was no matter. There were always more potential Hunters in the oceans of the word for the Mass to choose from.

The Mass was not self-aware, not in a way any human scientist would recognize, but it did possess a certain kind of intelligence. And as it floated in the ocean's calm silence, it felt something strange, something it had never felt before.

It felt an Other.

A mind, separate from itself. Smaller than its neural network, but *strong*. It was located not in the water, but on what the Mass thought of – inasmuch as it thought at all – as the Dry Which Does Not Move. The Mass was vaguely aware that there was food on the

Dry. From time to time over the millennia, its Hunters had snatched morsels from the Dry's edge or from the shallow waters close to the Dry. But there was so much more sustenance in the ocean that it rarely bothered going near the Dry. If it happened to drift close to shore, fine, but it didn't seek it out. As tasty as the food on the shore was, it wasn't worth the effort to go in search of it.

But this *Other* . . . There was something about its presence that called to the Mass, that pulled like the great tidal forces that moved the vast oceans themselves. The Other wasn't exactly like the Mass, but it was similar in many ways.

The Mass was intrigued.

The Mass wanted to investigate.

The Mass roused itself and floated to the surface. A moment later it began to drift slowly toward the Dry. Its Hunters, also awake now, swam forward, stretching their umbilicals as far as they would go, eager to see what they might find for their master.

CHAPTER THREE

The first thing Tamara did when she got back to her hotel room was take a shower. While she hadn't gone into the water today, she'd spent most of her time on the beach, shooting scenes or – far more often – waiting to shoot, and the saltwater air was *murder* on her hair. The Sea Breeze hotel, where the cast and crew of the production, Inez included, were staying was without exaggeration, the *shittiest* place Tamara had ever stayed in. The shower stall was cramped, the water lukewarm, and the entire bathroom smelled musty. Her allergies were *killing* her, and she was so loaded up on meds that she felt muzzy-headed all the time.

When she was finished, she dried herself and wrapped the towel around her head. She wished she had a joint to help her relax but carrying pot when you flew was such a hassle these days. She couldn't wait until it was finally legalized in all fifty states. Normally when she was on location, she had no problem obtaining weed. There were always locals hanging around who would do anything to get her to drop her panties. But so far she'd had no luck. It was that goddamned hurricane. Janice? Janeen? Something like that. It had fucked up Bridgewater pretty good a couple years ago, and now the place was practically a ghost town. She'd originally auditioned for the role of Holly, the "intelligent but sexy grad student," in this piece-of-crap movie because she thought it would get her some good publicity. Everyone was crazy about those dinosaurs that had eaten a bunch of people on that island, and Inez promised *Devourer from the Deep* would be the first movie based (however loosely) on that event.

People will go apeshit for it! Inez had told her. *We'll be on the cover of every magazine in the world!*

Tamara had known Inez was bullshitting her about how strongly people would react to her crappy low-budget monster movie, but she'd been willing to gamble that the film would be able to ride the current dino craze and garner some decent attention. But since signing the contract, Tamara hadn't been approached by a single reporter – not even a local one – for an interview. They'd only been in town shooting for several days, but she was already coming to regret landing this fucking role. She wanted to get through filming as fast as possible so she could go back to LA, buy some decent drugs, and start looking for another part. A *better* part. No more horror movies, though – and *definitely* no more working for Imagitopia Entertainment.

Something else that hadn't turned out the way she'd hoped was working with Jarrod Drayton. She'd seen a few of his films while growing up, and while she'd never been a huge fan, she'd enjoyed them well enough. But meeting Jarrod had been something of a disappointment. Oh, he was pleasant enough, but he had a sharp-edged wit that she wasn't fond of – especially when the pointed end of that wit was directed at her. Plus, he was gay. She had nothing against gay people. After all, she identified as pansexual. But Jarrod was *gay* gay. She'd tried flirting with him, had even "accidentally" lost her bikini top when the two of them had been alone once. Jarrod's eyes never dropped below the level of her chin. All he'd done was smile and say, *I believe you've dropped something, love.* So far in her career, she'd managed to fuck the lead actor in every film she'd had a part in, but now it looked like Jarrod was going to ruin her streak.

Show business could really be a downer sometimes.

She'd been sitting naked on her bed – except for the towel on her head, of course – for ten minutes or so when someone knocked at her door. She grinned, removed the towel from her head, gave her hair one last rub with it, then tossed it on the floor. She rose from the bed and padded barefoot over to the door. She'd could've peered through the peephole to see who was there, but what was the fun in that?

She opened the door. Pete Dawson stood there, wearing a pair of baggy shorts and an unbuttoned Hawaiian shirt. His gaze moved up and down her body, and when he got to her eyes, he smiled.

Tamara cocked a hip.

"Like what you see?" she asked.

"Oh yeah."

She stepped aside so Pete could enter, and once he was inside, she closed the door. The rooms opened directly to the outside, which meant it was possible someone might've seen him come in, but the risk turned Tamara on. Hell, if she thought she could convince Pete to go for it, she'd fuck him on the beach in broad daylight.

She went into Pete's arms and they kissed passionately. As they did, he worked her left breast with one hand and teased her clit with the other. She felt herself get instantly wet, and she began to relax. *This is exactly what the doctor ordered,* she thought. After a bit more, she pulled away and looked at him.

"How long do we have?" she asked.

"I told Shari that I was going back to the beach to talk to Enrique and see if the monster's going to be safe to work with tomorrow. I can stay out half an hour, easy. Maybe a little longer."

"Speaking of longer . . ."

Tamara slipped a hand inside Pete's shorts and began to knead his burgeoning erection. He closed his eyes and moaned with pleasure. Maybe she shouldn't be in such a hurry for this shoot to end. Not when she could find such pleasurable distractions as Pete.

A couple minutes later they were both naked on the bed and fucking like a pair of rabid weasels.

* * * * *

Jarrod – whose birth name was the decidedly non-sinister Carl Holmberg – lay on the bed in his room, staring up at a crack in the ceiling. Despite his nominally being the star of this production, his hotel room was no nicer or larger than the rest of the cast and crew had. This did not bother him overmuch, though. Back in the glorious eighties he'd been a bonafide star – at least to those audience members who loved horror films. Brutus, the insane killer in *The Ides of March* series, was his most famous role, but he starred in a dozen other films, usually portraying the villain but sometimes, more rarely, the hero. Some of his fans viewed him almost as a dark god, and like any actor, he ate up all the attention and adoration, and he would've been happy to keep doing so the rest of his life. Back then, he would've thrown a truly epic tantrum if he'd been forced to stay in a shithole like this during a shoot.

But the eighties hadn't been all good. He'd watched too many of his friends – and several lovers – sicken and die from AIDs. And more than once he thought he'd become infected too, but he'd never tested positive. He hadn't come out to the public at the time, although everyone in Hollywood knew he was gay. It wasn't until the late nineties, long after the height of his fame – such as it was – had passed that he told a writer interviewing him for a horror movie magazine that he was gay. When the article was printed, the reaction from fans was a collective shrug, which quite pleased him. The world still had plenty of intolerance in it, but it had seemed there was a bit less now.

He still had his fans, of course, and if they didn't number as many as they had during his heyday, their devotion made up for it. He made regular appearances at horror movie conventions around the country and sometimes overseas. And he still worked, although the productions became more modest – to put it kindly – with low budgets and mediocre-to-terrible scripts. But he was being paid to act, if not a king's ransom, and he was content with his lot.

He'd had relationships over the years, the longest lasting almost a decade, but he'd never found that special person, the one with whom he could grow old. And now he never would.

Leukemia was such an ugly word, but it was one he'd come to know extremely well over the last few years. Chemotherapy and radiation treatments had given him a short reprieve – nineteen months, to be precise – and then the disease had come raging back, worse than ever. The doctors had wanted him to go back into treatment immediately. They admitted his chances of going into remission again were slim, but slim was better than none, right?

Jarrod didn't see it that way. He'd be sixty-nine on his next birthday – assuming he lived long enough to reach it – and while that wasn't considered particularly old these days, he felt he'd had a good run overall, and besides, a true performer knew to always leave the audience wanting more. He'd made peace with his impending death and was – in a morbid way – rather looking forward to it. He didn't believe there was any life after this one, but who could say for certain until they crossed that final threshold?

He could do without the symptoms, though. Joint pain, dizziness, fatigue, fever, and general weakness were the worst, but loss of appetite was the most annoying. If he was dying, he should be allowed to eat anything he wanted. All the delicious fatty and sugary foods that he'd denied himself over the years to stay trim. But he didn't *want* to eat, had to practically force himself to nibble on something now and again. *There truly is no justice in this world,* he thought.

The doctors – who'd been surprisingly understanding of his choice – had prescribed medicine to make him comfortable as his disease continued to devour him from within. They couldn't say exactly how much time remained to him, but none of them expected him to live more than two more years, and that was the most optimistic estimate.

So who gave a shit about a crappy hotel room? He was alive in this moment, and he intended to enjoy it as much as possible. And he'd do the same with the next moment, and the one after that, and he'd keep doing it until there were no more moments left. His choice had come with an unanticipated benefit, though. He no longer gave a damn. He still cared about things – his work, his colleagues – but he was no longer afraid of doing or saying the wrong thing. In the face of death, that sort of piddly-ass shit was meaningless. He found this attitude delightfully freeing. It was one of the reasons he'd taken up smoking, and who knew what else he might do before the Reaper came knocking at his door? The world was his cancer-ridden oyster, and he intended to take full advantage of it while he could.

It was a shame that he'd had to start dying before he could truly live, but as the young people said, YO-fucking-LO.

He was grateful that the robo-dino had shit the bed this afternoon. He did his best to hide how tired he got these days from everyone, but even with drawing on his decades of experience lying for a living, he had a difficult time making it through a full day of filming without needing a rest. If he'd had a supporting role, he wouldn't be needed on set as often, but no, he'd taken the lead role, hadn't he? He might not be ego-driven as in his youth, but it seemed that even as he approached death, he still couldn't quite manage to give up the spotlight.

Vanity, thy name is actor.

He'd continue to lie here for a while, an hour, maybe two, and then he'd rise, make himself presentable – as much as he could. He'd lost weight because of his illness, and he had a pallor that, while perfectly appropriate for a horror movie actor, looked decidedly unhealthy on a regular human being. And, as he had every night since coming to this town, he'd hit Flotsam – one of the few bars still open in Bridgewater – select a table and hold court until the bar closed or he became too weary to continue, whichever came first.

He recalled something his grandmother, who'd continued working as a cleaning woman into her eighties, had once told him. *It's a good life if you don't weaken.*

"Damn straight, Gran," he said.

* * * * *

Tasha had the room next to Jarrod's, ostensibly so she'd be close if he needed anything. But he never called on her after the day's shooting was done. A dozen times each night she had to fight the urge to go knock on his door and ask if he needed anything. On the first day of shooting, when Inez had introduced her to Jarrod as his assistant, he'd said, *I promise to do my absolute best not to work you to death when we're filming, but when we're not shooting, your time is your own. You're too young to attend to an old relic like me night and day as if you were my personal servant. Go have fun. Take risks, make mistakes. Create some wonderfully embarrassing memories that you'll talk about for the rest of your life, laughing and crying at the same time.*

Tasha had loved that. It was *so* Jarrod Drayton. Witty, urbane, self-deprecating, and sentimental, the lines delivered in an avuncular, almost tongue-in-cheek style. But his words had also saddened her because she knew the real reason for them. He was dying, and other than Jarrod himself, she was the only one working on the film who knew it, including Inez.

Tasha sat on the floor, back against the wall, knees drawn to her chest, arms wrapped around her legs. This was the point in her room that was closest to where Jarrod was at the moment – lying on his bed – and while she didn't need to be this close physically to connect with him, it did make it easier.

The declining state of Jarrod's health should've been obvious to anyone with a functioning pair of eyes and a few working brain cells. But people in show business expected their colleagues to age poorly. Too much booze, drugs, cigarettes, and sun made anyone look older than they were. You were expected to look like shit if you survived to reach your golden years. It was almost a status symbol, evidence that you'd wrung every drop of pleasure out of your life and were still – at least some of the time – standing. So no one gave Jarrod's appearance – or how his energy began to flag as the day wore on – much thought. He'd managed to reach his twilight years more or less intact, and in the entertainment industry, that counted as a victory.

But Tasha knew the truth. She *always* knew.

She'd first realized she was different when she was two. Her mother had misplaced her wedding ring and was running around the house searching for it, frantic. Tasha didn't like seeing her mommy upset like that, so she took a quick peek into Mommy's mind to find the memory of where the ring was. Tasha didn't understand why people said they forgot things when the memories of every second they'd lived were stored in their brains, but for some reason, they couldn't access most of these memories. They just sat there in people's minds, unvisited and lonely. That made Tasha sad.

"Ring in the shower, Mommy," Tasha had said. Her vocabulary was far beyond her age, but this didn't bother Mommy or Daddy. They liked it, thought Tasha was a genius who was going to grow up to do great things someday. But when Mommy found the ring where Tasha said it would be – it was on the soap holder, right where Mommy had left it – she gave Tasha a funny look.

"How did you know where it was?" Mommy asked.

Tasha answered truthfully. "I can see inside your head."

Mommy frowned as she slipped her ring back onto her finger. Tasha could sense the emotions inside her mother – disbelief, wonder, excitement, but most of all, fear. Fear of Tasha, yes, but mostly it was fear *for* her.

"Thank you for finding my ring." Mommy smiled, but it was strained. "But you must be careful not to look inside other people's heads. It's not polite. People have a right to the privacy of their own thoughts. Do you understand?"

Tasha did, but even though Mommy had told her not to look, she had little control of her abilities yet. That would come later. So she saw the images in Mommy's mind, the ones that accompanied the thoughts she didn't want to speak aloud. Tasha on an operating table as doctors cut into her head to see how her brain worked. Men and women in uniforms telling her that it was her duty as a citizen to use her gifts for her country. People in business suits telling her she belonged to them now and she'd damn well better tell them what they wanted to know – about competitors, the stock market, the lottery, outcomes of sporting events . . . There were other images, too. People with wild eyes and angry expressions shouting *Freak! Witch! Demon!* People who would choke her, stab her, shoot her, kill her in any way they could as fast as they could because they were scared to death of her.

In that horrible, awful moment, Tasha understood that she was different than other people. Some would try to use her abilities for their own gain, some would seek to destroy her, but none of them would love her or value her or take care of her. Not like her mommy would.

Her mother never told her father about the ring, and from that day on, Tasha hid who she was and what she could do. She learned how not to look into people's minds, and when someone accidently projected a thought or emotion so strong she couldn't help but sense it, she pretended she didn't. And for the most part, she'd managed to live a relatively normal life. She'd remained alone for the most part. She couldn't have close friends, and she *especially* couldn't have lovers. She couldn't block the thoughts of people she became close to, no matter how hard she tried.

She'd had sex exactly once in her life, with Bobby Waters who lived down the street from her when they were both fifteen. One night when her parents were out, she invited Bobby over. She thought she might need to read his mind – if only a little – to find out how to make him want her, but it was unnecessary. He was a horny teen boy who got an erection whenever the wind blew, and he happily accepted her advances. The whole time he was thrusting in and out of her, he was mentally replaying violent sadomasochistic porn videos he watched on the Internet, only he imagined *her* face on the bodies of the women in the videos. Luckily, he came quickly, and she pushed him off her, got up, ran to the bathroom, and locked herself in. She vomited before she could reach the toilet, throwing up all over herself, the sink, and the floor.

The next day, still nauseated and suffering one of the worst headaches of her life, she sat on the couch in her PJ's watching TV. Her mom assumed she was having a bad period and gave her some medicine to take and a heating pad for her nonexistent cramps. Tasha zoned out as she watched whatever was on the screen, feeling miserable and, not for the first time, contemplating suicide, when Jarrod Drayton entered her life.

The movie was called *The Mindkillers*, and Jarrod played a psychic who battled a group of extra-dimensional entities that fed on people's thoughts and emotions the same way vampires fed on blood. The film was cheesy, but Tasha had never seen someone like her portrayed as a hero before, and watching Jarrod defeat the Mindkillers cheered her up considerably. She'd fallen in love with Jarrod that day. Not in a sexual way, but in a deeper, truer way. He'd become a symbol for her, a role model of sorts, showing her that not only was there nothing wrong or bad about her, but that she was actually special and could do important things if she wanted.

She became Jarrod Drayton's biggest fan after that. She watched all his movies over and over, read or watched every interview with him she could find, collected every item of Jarrod Drayton memorabilia she could get, plastered the walls of her bedroom with posters and photos of Jarrod. She'd even gotten a tattoo of the logo for *The Mindkillers* across her shoulders. After she graduated from high school, she went to a college near her hometown in Ohio and majored in film history and criticism. She wrote papers about Jarrod's movies, even made a documentary about him for one of her classes.

And during her senior year, only a couple of months before graduation, she learned Jarrod was going to be making an appearance at a horror convention only six hours from her school. She had to hustle to scrape up the money to go, but she managed – her parents helped – and she drove to the convention, paid her entry fee, and made her way to where the celebrities in attendance sat at a table, chatting with fans, signing photos, and taking selfies with them. Most of the celebrities charged for signatures and photos – some of them quite a bit – but not Jarrod.

She'd almost chickened out at the last moment. What if he turned out to be an asshole or a perv? She would be crushed if she discovered the Jarrod Drayton she'd come to love and almost worship existed only in her imagination. But she made herself go up and talk to him, and she quickly relaxed. He was kind, sweet, and good-humored, and although she didn't pry into his thoughts, she could sense he was a good person. Unfortunately, she also sensed he was ill – seriously so – and this knowledge hit her like a punch to the gut. She could no longer resist peering into his mind then. She *had* to know what was wrong with him. So she looked, and she learned about his leukemia, and how he was done fighting the disease. He'd accepted his fate and was at peace with it, and that helped her accept it, too. But she also learned that in the summer, he would be shooting a film in Texas. His last film. And right there and then, she decided she had to be a part of the crew, no matter what.

She gleaned all the specifics she needed from his mind, and after she graduated, she moved to LA, visited Imagitopia Entertainment's offices, and – using her abilities – said all the right things. That got her an unpaid internship, which meant she did whatever scut work needed doing around the building. But with her abilities, it didn't take long for her to learn that Inez Perry was the one to talk to about getting on the crew of *Devourer from the Deep*. And so one day she simply went into Inez's office, said the right things that persuaded Inez's assistant to let her pass, and then she introduced her to Inez and said the right things that landed her a job – an extremely low-paying one – as Jarrod's personal assistant during the filming of the movie.

She wanted to spend as much time with Jarrod as she could before he died, wanted to learn everything about filmmaking that he could teach her. But most of all, she wanted to get to know him as a person and not as an actor or the characters he portrayed.

Now her dream had come true, and while it was everything she'd hoped for, it came with something that she hadn't anticipated. The more time she spent in Jarrod's presence, the stronger her psychic bond to him became. There was a deep well of loneliness at the core of Jarrod's being – and while she could identify with this, for she had a similar loneliness inside her – it hurt to feel it all the time. And while Jarrod might tell himself he wasn't afraid of dying, and on some level believed it, on a deeper level he was terrified, as she suspected all beings were when they knew the end of their life was drawing close. She felt this fear in addition to his loneliness, and together they were almost more than she could bear. In a way, it felt like she was dying, too.

But she was determined to endure. She wouldn't abandon Jarrod, no matter how hard it was to remain close to him. She needed him in a way that she didn't fully understand. And she would do what she could to alleviate some of his loneliness. No one should die alone, and she would not abandon him, no matter the cost to herself.

So she sat on the floor, feeling Jarrod's mind through the wall that separated them. And when he finally got back enough strength to go to Flotsam, she'd wait a few minutes – so it wouldn't be too obvious – and then she'd follow. And she'd spend the night in the presence of her hero, doing what she could to take away a little of his loneliness and fear, at least for a short while.

But something besides Jarrod's illness gnawed at her mind. When she'd brought him a cigarette on the beach earlier, she'd sensed . . . well, she wasn't sure exactly *what* she'd sensed. A presence of some sort, a living thing in the water near the shore. A *big* thing. At first she'd thought it was an animal of some kind, most likely a whale. But she'd touched thousands of animal minds in her life – the main reason she was a vegetarian – but she'd never experienced anything like this. Animal thoughts were simpler than those of humans for the most part, but the presence she felt was a strange combination of simple and complex. Its mind was far larger than any she'd ever touched before. There was a great deal of communication happening between its various parts. But that communication was extremely basic, kind of like the signals sent back and forth through a central nervous system. It was as if she had sensed the most sophisticated neural network that had ever evolved, but there was no mind attached to it.

Its thoughts, such as they were, sounded to her mind like the buzzing of a million insects, orderly but utterly inhuman. But as alien as this presence was, what disturbed her the most was the impulse that motivated it more than any other: hunger. It was always hungry, had always been so, and never in its long, long life had it been satiated. Not once. In its own way, she found this as sad as she did Jarrod's loneliness. Its hunger was so strong, it was almost overwhelming. But even though she'd tried, she'd been unable to sense what the presence hungered for. And that frightened her.

A *lot*.

CHAPTER FOUR

After Inez dismissed the cast and crew, she returned to where Saul and Boyd were standing. They'd continued talking in low voices while she'd told everyone they could go, and now that she was coming back, they broke off their conversation and turned to look at her, both of their faces masks of innocence. She knew they'd been complaining about her behind her back. She'd have been disappointed if they hadn't. Her job wasn't to make friends. It was to ensure that Imagitopia's films got made on time without going over their meager budgets. This was why she insisted on being on set during a shoot. She wanted to keep an eye on things, make sure directors didn't film too many takes and that actors showed up on time and reasonably clear-headed. And if she had to be an overbearing bitch to get the job done, then so be it. She'd produced fifty-seven films for Imagitopia in her career, and while none of them had been award-winners or major hits at the box office, she liked to think they were solid pieces of entertainment.

Inez *loved* movies, had ever since her parents had taken her to see *The Wizard of Oz* on the big screen during a classic film series at a local cinema when she was a child. Of all the art forms in the world, movies were the most magical. They had the ability to draw audiences into a story unlike anything else, and they could reach millions, even billions of people, moving hearts and changing minds across the planet. Inez's love for film was wide-ranging and unconditional for one simple reason: she had no critical faculties. A rowdy sex comedy which made almost no money was, in her mind, equal to a grand historical drama that swept all the awards the year it was released. She wasn't deluded, though. She understood that some films were better than others, but she found some measure of enjoyment in watching all of them. It was this quality – her love of movies regardless of how great or shitty they might be – which made her so excellent at what she did. She knew a film didn't have to be a great work of cinematic art or cost a trillion fucking dollars to make to be good.

So let people complain about what a tightwad she was when it came to a film's budget, and let directors bitch that she didn't understand their "vision." As far as she was concerned, *she* was the one who really made the magic happen, and she was determined to do the same for *Devourer from the Deep* – even if their Devourer itself was, at the moment, mechanically indisposed.

When she rejoined Saul and Boyd, she said, "Tell me your brilliant ideas for working around our disabled friend over there." She nodded to the mechanical pliosaur, whose inner works Enrique continued to examine while muttering a string of profanities.

Saul and Boyd exchanged uneasy looks.

"It's kind of hard to shoot a monster movie without a monster," Saul said.

Boyd nodded.

"We'll have our monster," Inez said. "Don't worry about that. The question is how *much* of it we'll have and how well it will work. What I need from both of you are ideas of how to rework scenes so that we shoot them with minimal effects while still keeping them scary and suspenseful."

"I'm not sure that's necessary," Boyd said. His hipster glasses slipped down on his nose, and he pushed them back. It was a nervous habit he had, and it drove Inez nuts. "We can shoot the scenes as written, and you can put in the effects shots later using CGI."

Saul rolled his eyes. "Here we go."

Boyd had never worked with Inez before. If he had, he'd have known better than to make that suggestion. Inez spoke slowly, as if she were a teacher addressing a child who was having difficulty following a lesson.

"Those kind of effects cost *money*. And they take *time* to create. We need to finish our film and get it out ASAP, while everyone's still excited about those dinosaurs."

"Pliosaurs aren't technically dinosaurs," Boyd said.

Inez blinked several times. "Excuse me?"

"They're reptiles. Distant cousins of turtles, actually." He smiled. "I pride myself on my research."

Inez scowled as she tried to determine if Boyd was somehow making fun of her.

"They have *saur* in their name, don't they?" she said. "That makes them dinosaurs as far as I'm concerned."

Boyd opened his mouth to respond, but Saul put a hand on his shoulder and shook his head. Boyd got the message and shut his mouth.

Inez gave Boyd a slow, dangerous smile. "Tell me, Boyd. Given your *vast* professional experience, do you think it's normal for a writer to be present during a shoot?"

"Uh . . ." Boyd looked to Saul for help, but the director had turned his attention to a nearby gull that was trying to dig something out of the sand with its beak.

Inez continued. "It is *not* normal. But I always invite writers to my sets. And I do it for reasons like that." She stabbed a finger toward the inoperable pliosaur. "Things happen on set, things you can't always plan for. And that sometimes means the script will need some tweaking to work around whatever problem has arisen. Your entire purpose for being here is to tweak the script when I tell you it needs tweaking. Do you understand?"

Boyd nodded, a trifle sullenly, she thought.

"Good. Now I want you to go back to your room, fire up your laptop, and do what?"

"Tweak," Boyd said in a small, miserable voice.

"That's right," Inez said, almost purring. "I want you to tweak like a sonofabitch."

* * * * *

"Fuck, fuck, *fuck!*"

Enrique smacked the side of the mechanical pliosaur – which he'd nicknamed Bob – in frustration. He'd built the goddamned thing, and he'd done the best he could with the budget he'd been given. But he hadn't been able to insulate the inner mechanism the way he would've liked, and as a result, the saltwater was playing merry hob with Bob's guts, turning him into an expensive, but useless, statue.

Enrique stood in the water next to Bob, the waves rolling into shore surging high enough to reach his waist at times. There was no way he'd be able to fix Bob here in the water – if the fucking thing could be fixed at all. Bob was currently attached to a wheeled wooden platform to make him mobile, the platform designed so that once the wheels were removed, the pliosaur could be towed behind a boat for open-water scenes. If Enrique had had a decent budget to work with, Bob would've been mounted on a sleek foundation made of fiberglass. But he'd had what he'd had, and the wooden platform would serve, provided they didn't tow it too fast. Otherwise, their aquatic dinosaur would be in danger of capsizing.

This morning, Lee Fleming, a local tow-truck driver – *Big-Time Tow: Bridgewater's Best!* – had come out to help put Bob into the water, and she was scheduled to return at dusk. Enrique would have her take Bob to the empty warehouse Inez had rented for the production's equipment storage. Once Bob was inside, Enrique could peel back the pliosaur's rubber skin and let the machinery inside air dry overnight. Who knows? Maybe that would be enough to get the damn thing working again.

Yeah, and maybe a hundred of Bob's flesh-and-blood cousins will swim out of my ass, he thought.

As he rubbed his hand across Bob's rubber hide, he marveled that a creature such as this was actually real. He'd seen the videos of the killings on *Las Dagas*. Who hadn't? They were all over the net. And like everyone else, he'd read all the articles about the pliosaurs that had attacked the island resort of Elysium. He knew pliosaurs – long thought extinct with the rest of the dinosaurs – still lived in the modern day, but he couldn't quite make himself believe it.

He became aware of Inez approaching, and he groaned inwardly. He did not need any of her shit right now. She stopped when she reached the edge of the water. The entire time they'd been here, Enrique had never seen her so much as dip a toe into the ocean.

"So?" she said. "What's the verdict?"

The verdict is you're a goddamned penny pincher who won't give the people you employ the resources they need to do the job.

Aloud, he said, "The works are gummed up from the saltwater. They might function after they've had a chance to dry off." He shrugged. "They might not."

Inez's face darkened.

"If you can't guarantee the monster – which, by the way, is the *real* star of this movie – will function, then what the fuck am I paying you for?"

Enrique gritted his teeth. He wanted to turn to Inez and tell her where she could shove her precious monster, but instead he put his hands back inside Bob and pretended to tinker some more. Inez was the Queen of the Ballbusters, but he didn't want to piss her off. Any more than she already was, that is.

When it came to special effects, Enrique was a throwback. He loved practical effects and believed they were far superior to CGI. Yeah, CGI allowed for greater flexibility. You could make a CGI-rendered character move in all sorts of ways. But Enrique thought CGI looked flat and cartoonish, entirely unconvincing. It had no tactile reality, no sense of presence, no *there*. And since the actors had nothing solid to react to, their performances lacked authenticity. Enrique was on a one-man crusade to convince people in the industry and the audience who viewed their films of the superiority of practical effects.

Inez was one of the few producers left who remained open to the use of practical effects, who didn't think they were interchangeable with CGI. He didn't know if this was an aesthetic preference of Inez's or – and he thought this far more likely – she didn't know much about CGI and assumed anything to do with computers was hideously expensive. Whichever the case, most of the films Enrique worked on these days were Imagitopia productions, and if he wanted to keep working, he had to stay on Inez's good side.

"So you're telling me that I'm going to have to wait an entire *day* to see if this goddamned thing will work or not," she said.

"More or less."

Enrique knew Inez hated wasting time on a shoot. Time was money, and money was one thing Imagitopia didn't have a lot of. Plus, she was determined that her pliosaur movie hit the market before any other could be released. Delay was simply unacceptable. Unfortunately, in this case, it was also unavoidable.

Enrique thought Inez would continue berating him, but instead she let out a weary sigh.

"I've spoken with Saul and Boyd about reworking the pliosaur attack scenes in the script to make them less . . . ambitious. If your oversized wind-up toy doesn't start working again, I figure we can remove the head and flippers and use them like puppets."

Enrique stopped pretending to work on Bob and turned an incredulous face toward Inez.

"Puppets?"

"Sure. You remove any metal parts from them so they're not too heavy, and we con a couple of the locals into helping us. They can slap the flippers against the water, thrust the head at the actors, that sort of thing. As long as we're careful in how we film the monster scenes – and if we're clever in how we edit the footage – it'll work. It's not like I haven't done it before."

Enrique couldn't restrain himself any longer.

"It'll look like shit," he said.

Inez didn't seem to be offended in the slightest.

"You know Imagitopia's unofficial motto as well as I do: 'It doesn't have to be good, it just has to get done.' How long would it take you to get the head and flippers ready?"

Enrique hated Inez's idea. It was the kind of thing that made practical effects – and those who created them – look ridiculous. Still, he thought for a moment and then said, "A few hours."

"Fuck it. Go ahead and do it." Before Enrique could protest, she said, "*If* you get the machine working again, you can always put the head and flippers back on. But in the meantime, we'll keep shooting."

Enrique didn't like it, but he knew his feelings didn't matter. Inez would do what she'd do, and it was up to him to either get with the program or get the fuck out of the way.

"Fine," Enrique said, managing not to sound too discouraged. "The tow truck will be here around dusk, and we'll get Bob to the warehouse. I'll start working on removing the head and flippers. They'll be ready to use by tomorrow morning."

Inez grinned. "Excellent! This is why I love working with you, Enrique. You're always so accommodating."

Don't say anything, he warned himself. *Don't say anything.*

There was still plenty of daylight left, and if he got started now, he might be able to finish before dark. Then he could join the others at Flotsam where he could drink and bitch about Inez to his heart's content. But until then, he had to keep being a good boy.

He started walking toward shore, intending to go to his rented pickup to get his tools, when there came a loud *thump* and Bob shuddered, as if something large had struck him.

Enrique frowned. *What the hell was that?* It couldn't have been a wave. Bob's head was pointed toward shore, and whatever had hit him had done so on his right side. Besides, waves made slapping sounds when they hit something, not thumps. Something solid had struck Bob. Solid and *big*.

"Get out of the water, Enrique."

Inez's voice was completely devoid of emotion, almost as if she was in shock. Her tone frightened him more than her words did, but instead of running onto the beach, he froze. He looked around frantically, trying to see what Inez had warned him about. At first he saw nothing, but then a shark fin emerged from the water less than twenty feet from where he stood. It was followed by a second fin, and both of them moved quickly toward him. The fins were gray, shot through with crimson threads that reminded him of veins. He'd never seen a shark up close outside of an aquarium, and he'd never seen one with red striations like these.

As the fins drew closer, their paths diverged. One veered off while the other continued toward him. He watched its approach with fascination. Several years ago, he'd done the effects for an Imagitopia film called *Shark Wars*, and he'd spent a lot of time reading about sharks and watching documentaries about them. He prided himself on his accuracy to detail, and he'd wanted to make sure the shark effects in the film looked as convincing as possible.

The detail he liked best was how the fins sliced through the water, smooth and quiet, as if they were moving through air. The sharks he'd made for *Shark War* hadn't quite been able to move like that, and he'd hoped he'd get another chance to work on a shark film in the future, so he'd get another shot at –

The shark coming toward him shot out of the water as if it had been launched by a catapult. He recognized it as a bull shark – a big one – and he wasn't surprised to see crimson veins running through its entire body. He had time to note two other strange details in the last few seconds of his life. The shark's eyes were completely red, as if they were filled with blood, and something like an umbilical cord – also red – was attached to its body behind the fin, the other end stretching down into the water.

Man, that is a fantastic fucking design! he thought.

The shark slammed into Enrique, jaws fastening on his head. Blood gushed from the wounds, and the impact snapped his neck, killing him before the shark's weight bore his body down into the water.

* * * * *

Imagitopia produced films other than horror. Actions films and low-brow comedies, mostly. Sci-fi, too, if the effects the script called for weren't too expensive. But horror was the company's bloody bread and butter. Inez – who was an admitted control freak – had been on the sets of dozens of horror films in her career. She'd watched scenes of torture, murder, and dismemberment without batting an eye, witnessed gallons of fake blood splashing everywhere. Because of this, she thought seeing real violence would have little effect on her. But when she saw the shark jump out of the water and practically bite off Enrique's head in a spray of real blood, she realized that she hadn't known shit about real violence.

The shark took Enrique down into the water and began thrashing its head back and forth, tossing around Enrique's body until his head finally came loose. The shark then let go of the head, fastened its jaws onto his torso and withdrew, pulling the body back into the ocean until they were both lost to sight.

It had happened so fast that Inez had been unable to do more than watch open mouthed as Enrique was killed and then dragged away to be eaten. She hadn't even possessed the presence of mind to scream. But now, almost as if she were coming out of a hypnotic trance, she drew in a breath, intending to release the loudest, strongest scream of her life. Before she could, however, she noticed a second red-veined fin gliding toward the beach. It was heading in her direction at first, but then it changed course and headed for the mechanical pliosaur, which Enrique – dead and likely being devoured this very moment – had dubbed Bob.

What the hell was the shark doing? Did it think the pliosaur was real, a potential food source or maybe even a competitor, and wanted to investigate? Despite producing a number of shark-attack movies, Inez had no real idea how the fish hunted. Smell? Vibrations in the water? Something else? Whatever drove the shark onward, it surged toward Bob and, just as its companion had, it leaped out of the water to attack. It had the same weird red veins threaded through its hide, same red eyes, and the same umbilical cord as the other had. Also like the first shark, it aimed for Bob's head. Unfortunately for the shark, instead of bone, muscle, and organs, beneath Bob's exterior lay a sturdy metal frame and heavy hydraulic equipment. The shark slammed into Bob's head with such force that rubber tore and the metal frame bent, forcing the pliosaur's head sideways. The shark fared much worse. Its head exploded in a shower of blood and meat, and it flipped over, flew through the air, and landed on the beach less than two yards from where Inez stood.

She wasn't afraid of being bitten, for the shark's head had been reduced to a ragged, blood-soaked mess. Its killing days were over. Bob 1, Shark 0.

The umbilicus which trailed back into the water pulsed with a regular rhythm, almost like a heart beating. It lay motionless on the sand for a moment before pulling free from the shark's abdomen with a sickeningly wet tearing sound. Meat tore, blood flowed, and Inez saw the umbilicus terminated in a wicked-looking barb. The cord then rose upward and began swaying back and forth, like a serpent trying to mesmerize its prey. It was at this point that the part of Inez's mind dedicated to self-preservation took over. She turned and started to run, but before she could get more than a few feet, the barb shot toward her and embedded itself into the base of her spine. The impact sent her sprawling face-first, and she lay on the sand as the Mass took control of her.

* * * * *

The Mass had moved as close to shore as it dared. Its leading edge was practically beached, but the majority of its body remained afloat. The Hunter that survived brought the headless body of the man to the Mass, and it absorbed the meat and bone greedily. The second Hunter had died, but this did not concern the Mass. Hunters were always temporary, and it made no difference to the Mass if its servants died sooner or later, from accidents or natural causes. The Mass had existed for millions of years. Everything besides itself and the ocean it had inhabited was fleeting, of no real importance.

The umbilici that the Mass used to attach Hunters to itself came loose when a Hunter died and immediately sought out a new host. Whatever suitable lifeform was closest would do until such time as a more appropriate Hunter – such as a shark – could be found. The umbilicus of the dead Hunter had done what it was designed to do, and it had found a new host. But for the first time in the Mass' long, long life, an umbilicus had attached itself to a creature of the Dry. And not just any creature, but one with a far more developed mind than any the Mass had ever bonded with before.

The Mass instinctively understood that this creature would not make an efficient Hunter. It was weak and slow, its flesh soft and vulnerable. What's more, its small, flat teeth were useless for grabbing and holding onto prey – and it couldn't breathe underwater. Still, there was something about this softskin: the Mass had ingested many of its kind over the millennia, but it had never joined with one before. The softskin's mind was far more complex than those of its current Hunters. For all their strengths, shark were simple, instinct-driven creatures. They possessed an elegantly deadly design which made them supreme hunters in the ocean, yes, but they added nothing to the Mass' vast neural network. This softskin had large quantities of information stored in its sophisticated brain, and for the first time in the Mass' unimaginably long life, it realized there were other ways to feed besides ingesting meat. It could ingest knowledge as well.

The Mass commanded the softskin to walk into the surf, and the creature had no choice but to comply. When it was up to its chest in water, the Mass commanded it to stop. The Mass sent a Hunter to the softskin, and when the crimson-veined shark was close enough, the softskin took hold of its dorsal fin, and the Hunter began swimming out to sea, bearing the softskin toward the main body of the Mass. And when it arrived, the Mass would feed in a way it had never fed before.

The Mass was incapable of experiencing emotion, but its neural network jangled with a sensation not unlike excitement.

CHAPTER FIVE

When Inez returned to consciousness, she found herself in darkness.

She didn't panic. She simply assumed she was in her hotel room, and the lights were off. She had absolutely no memory of how she'd gotten here. The last thing she remembered was talking to Saul and Boyd about script revisions, and then . . . There was nothing. It had been late afternoon when she'd spoken with Saul and Boyd, and given how dark it was in her room – pitch-fucking-black, actually – it had to be nighttime. What had happened in the intervening hours? Had she gone to Flotsam and gotten utterly shitfaced? Normally she was careful to drink in moderation during a shoot, but when the liquor began flowing, she would often wax nostalgic and start relating anecdotes about her time in the business, and after that she'd begin telling scandalous stories about the sexcapades of various industry notables. If she wasn't careful she'd keep gabbing and drinking until she was drunk off her ass by closing time. That's probably what had happened this time, and while it was embarrassing, it was hardly unprecedented. The *real* question was whether she'd come back to her room alone or if she had a guest or two lying next to her. It wouldn't be the first time, and while some people could manage to be adult about such situations come morning, sometimes they made for awkwardness and hurt feelings on set. It was her job to make sure everything went as smoothly as possible during filming, not to create problems by fucking the wrong person – or people – when she was blind stinking drunk.

She considered saying to hell with it and going back to sleep and dealing with the fallout of whatever mistake she'd made in the morning. But she decided she'd rather find out what she was in for now. She reached out her hand, but her fingers didn't come in contact with another body. She felt a wave of relief until she realized something. She'd only *thought* she'd reached out. She hadn't actually moved at all.

She felt a sting of panic then, and she tried to move once more. Nothing difficult, just raising her right hand off the bed. She felt nothing, so she concentrated harder, but she still didn't feel anything. She couldn't feel her body, not any part of it. She didn't feel numb, either. Numbness was a sensation, and she felt absolutely nothing. She tried to draw in a breath but couldn't. She listened for her heartbeat but heard nothing.

Oh god. I'm dead.

Her missing memories came flooding back to her then. She remembered speaking with Enrique about the mechanical pliosaur, remembered the strange shark that had attacked and killed him. Remembered the one that killed itself trying to attack the pliosaur, remembered its umbilicus detaching and waving around, as if searching for something else to attach to.

Me. It attached to me.

What had happened after that was still hazy, as if she'd experienced it in a waking dream state. Another of those weird sharks swam her out to sea, to a large island of some kind, its surface red and crusty, as if it was a gigantic scab. She'd climbed out of the water and onto the island, and she'd begun walking, the rough surface giving beneath her feet as she went, as if it wasn't earth but rather living tissue. And then an orifice had opened before her, and she stepped into it. Once inside, it closed around her, sealing out the light, and after that there was nothing until she'd woken in the darkness, her body gone. Digested? Maybe. But the most important part of her remained – her mind. Was she now nothing but a brain housed somewhere within whatever the hell this thing was? Or had she been reduced to . . . what? A network of electrical impulses which combined to create the consciousness that thought of itself as Inez Perry?

She supposed it didn't matter. Whatever she was, she was part of this thing – the island – the shark had brought her to. She could sense it. She wondered what else she could sense, and she concentrated on calming herself, on lowering her mental defenses and allowing information to come into her. It wasn't a gradual process. It came upon her in an instant, a vast sea of data that rolled over her with tsunami force. It was so overwhelming that for a time she lost her sense of self. But eventually it returned, and when it did, she understood what had happened. The Mass – a creature that had traveled the world's oceans since the dawn of time – had absorbed her. Not as food, but rather as a kind of operating system. The goddamned thing had given itself an upgrade. For the first time in millions of years the Mass was self-aware. It had consciousness. It had *her*.

It seemed she had become a monster.

Rather than being dismayed by this thought, she was excited. The Mass had for the most part been doing the same thing the same way since it sent out its first umbilicus to snag its first Hunter, a little tadpole-like creature swimming in a stagnant prehistoric pond. The Mass had grown since then, and now it was as big as the largest whale, and then some. But it was in a rut, and the poor thing hadn't known it. Until now, that is.

She thought of the film she'd been making. *Devourer from the Deep* meant nothing to her anymore. She no longer had use for pretend monsters. Now *she* was a monster, and she intended to put on a show the like of which the world had never seen. But first, she needed to do a bit more upgrading. The Hunters had been more than sufficient for the Mass' needs before she'd come along, but they lacked versatility and – just as important – style. The Mass had never considered using its capabilities, which were considerable, to make changes to its Hunters, but that's exactly what Inez intended to do. She had something the Mass hadn't possessed before – imagination. And it was a tool the Mass could make good use of. Oh yes, it was.

Whatever she now was – disembodied brain, chemically stored information, a small network of electrical impulses housed inside a much larger one – it was the Mass that was ultimately in charge. It had one all-encompassing, overriding need: to eat, and that's what she would help it do. But eating didn't have to be boring, did it? It could be fun, too, and Inez intended to teach the Mass exactly what fun was. She would make a movie – a *horror* movie. The most spectacular ever created, because it wouldn't just be a movie. It would be real.

Goddamn, this was going to be fun!

She sent out a mental command and a complex mix of enzymes began flowing through the umbilical cords into the Hunters.

And they began to change.

CHAPTER SIX

"*The Ides of March VII* was my favorite. The makeup was fantastic!"

Bonnie Choi – the *Devourer from the Deep*'s one and only makeup artist – sat next to Jarrod. She was of Korean descent, and for reasons Jarrod didn't know but absolutely loved anyway, she never wore makeup herself. As far as he was concerned, she didn't need it. The natural look suited her. She wore shorts, flip flops, and a *Devourer from the Deep* T-shirt. Jarrod was getting sick of looking at those damn shirts.

Most of the cast and crew had gathered in Flotsam, a hole-in-the-wall beachside bar less than a mile from the Sea Breeze Hotel. The place was so close to the ocean, Jarrod had no idea how it had survived the fury of Hurricane Janae when so many of the buildings around it hadn't. Flotsam looked like any other small-town bar Jarrod had ever seen. Wooden floor, tables, chairs, bar with stools and a brass foot rail, dim lighting, TV on the wall – currently tuned to a tennis match with the sound muted. The sole nod to individuality was the decorative items on the walls. They were, as the establishment's name suggested, items that had been washed up onto the beach. An old-fashioned key, a number of shoes, a hockey puck, an honest-to-god bottle with a message in it (written in Japanese and so far untranslated), a plastic duck, a rusted machete, and more. Jarrod supposed the objects were intended to give the place a funky, eclectic vibe, but it merely looked cluttered and random to him, like someone's attic had exploded.

There were few locals here tonight – a half dozen or so – and those who were present had been employed to work on the film as grips and such. Manual labor hired for cheap. They were lovely people, and Jarrod hoped they enjoyed working on the film since they damn sure weren't getting rich from it.

Besides Bonnie, Jarrod's tablemates for this evening consisted of Tasha (seated on his right), Saul, and Pete Dawson. Troy Jennings and Nina Katri sat at the table next to theirs. The remaining members of the film's crew – Inez, Boyd, Enrique, Tamara, and Shari Dawson – were absent. No doubt Inez had chained Boyd to his computer for the evening so he could do rewrites for tomorrow, the poor sonofabitch. Writers were always shit on in Hollywood. He assumed the others would be along in time. With perhaps the exception of Tamara. Her sexual appetites were legendary – so much so that Jarrod was more than a little jealous of her – and she might be entertaining a visitor (or more) in her room right now. He briefly wondered if she was with Boyd and decided it wasn't likely. He hadn't noticed her flirting with the writer at any time during the few days they'd been filming. Inez then? Highly doubtful. Inez swung that way now and again, but she tried to avoid screwing anyone who worked on one of her pictures. Not until after filming had wrapped, anyway. Enrique? Perhaps. The man *was* quite attractive. If Jarrod had been a couple decades younger . . .

Bonnie spoke once again, pulling Jarrod away from his thoughts.

"Nigel Stanford did the makeup on that movie, didn't he? How in the hell did you get an Academy Award-winning makeup artist to work on a film like *that?*" She stopped then, her cheeks coloring from embarrassment. "I'm sorry. I didn't mean to imply *Ides of March VII* wasn't . . . uh . . ."

Jarrod laughed.

"No need to apologize, my dear. *The Ides of March* series might've been popular in its time, but it was hardly high art. The reason Nigel took the job was simple: we were lovers at the time, and he did it as a favor to me. We broke up soon after, actually. Nigel's reputation took a hit after he worked on the film, and it became a sore point between us. We argued about it, and one thing led to another . . ." Jarrod shrugged. "We were young and foolish." *As if that's an excuse,* he thought.

He was drinking a whiskey sour, and he downed the remainder of it and held up the empty to signal to the bartender that he wanted another.

"Maybe you should have something to eat first," Tasha said.

Jarrod put on a smile.

"Thanks for your concern, love, but I ate in my room before coming over."

Tasha opened her mouth as if she were about to call him on his lie, but she said nothing. She didn't look happy, though.

Jarrod wasn't irritated by Tasha looking out for him. He found it rather sweet, actually. But he could hardly tell her that the thought of taking even a single bite of food was repellent to him. For some reason – one for which he was profoundly grateful – his lack of appetite didn't extend to alcohol. If it had, he wouldn't have been getting any calories at all.

There was something off about Tasha tonight, although he couldn't have said what it was. She seemed preoccupied, even withdrawn, as if her mind was elsewhere. He hoped it wasn't anything he'd done or said. She turned to him then and smiled reassuringly, as if she read his mind. Before meeting her, he would've found the notion ridiculous. But now . . . She was drinking diet soda. She'd told him she didn't like the effect alcohol had on her. Jarrod had wondered exactly what effect she'd been referring to, but he hadn't wanted to pry.

Saul was drinking scotch and water (and very little of the latter), although he mostly held his glass in his hand and stared down at it. He seemed discouraged, almost depressed. Jarrod suspected he knew why. Early in his own career, he'd find himself feeling down in the middle of a shoot when he realized the film he was working on was a piece of shit, and despite his best efforts, there was nothing he could do to make it better. Jarrod had learned to deal with this by focusing on doing the best work he was capable of given the circumstances, knowing that there was an appreciative audience out there for these kind of films, regardless of how "good" they might be according to critics' standards.

Jarrod didn't think sharing this insight with Saul would do any good, though. Saul was a man who, despite his years in the industry, still had ambitions. He didn't want to spend the rest of his career making cheap horror movies, but Jarrod suspected that Saul was beginning to realize that at this point in his life, it was a very real possibility that he would end up doing precisely that. Jarrod wished he could teach the man the sacred art of No Longer Giving a Fuck, but considering he'd had to contract a fatal disease to learn it himself, he doubted it was something that could be taught.

Too bad. I'd make a killing as a self-help guru otherwise.

Pete had barely said more than a handful of words since sitting down. He had a mug of beer which he periodically took sips of, but he spent the majority of his time sneaking glances at the door. Was he anxious for Shari's arrival? Or perhaps someone else's?

The bartender came over with Jarrod's new drink, and he exchanged his empty glass for the full one.

"Last night you were drinking mojitos. Why the change up?"

Susan Holland was both owner and head bartender of Flotsam, and if Jarrod had been straight, he'd have fallen in love with her. He was a bit in love with her anyway. She was a tall, athletic, short-haired brunette in her late thirties. She was heavily tattooed with intricate tribal designs, and she had a nose ring and multiple piercings in each ear, including expanders. She was a runner and ran marathons all over the country. She'd told Jarrod that Flotsam's sole purpose as far as she was concerned was to finance her running career. But if she resented having to work to support her running habit, it didn't show. She was always pleasant and had a sarcastic attitude that Jarrod adored. Tonight, she wore cowboy boots – hardly conducive to running, Jarrod thought – jeans, and a black concert T-shirt for a band he'd never heard of: Infant Annihilator.

"I dislike mixing drinks, and I despise being predictable," Jarrod said. "Sticking with a different drink each night is a good compromise between the two."

Susan grinned.

"As long as you keep buying drinks, it's all good as far as I'm concerned." She addressed the rest of the table then. "Anyone else need anything?" No one did, so she moved off to check on her other customers.

Sudden warmth came over Jarrod, along with lightheadedness. *A fever,* he thought. A symptom of his leukemia. Unpleasant, but nothing to be alarmed about. It hit him like this sometimes, full on when he least expected it. All he had to do was ride it out and he'd be fine. It might last a short time or continue for the rest of the night, but eventually it would end. Although in the meantime he was hardly going to be the life of the party.

He felt Tasha's feather-light touch as she placed her hand atop one of his. She tightened her grip slightly, and before he could ask what she was doing, he felt his fever recede. No, that wasn't right. The fever was still there, he knew that, but he didn't feel it as strongly anymore. It was as if the circuitry in his brain that connected his consciousness to his fever had been switched off.

He turned his hand over beneath Tasha's and gave her a gentle squeeze.

Thank you, he thought, and he was not at all surprised when Tasha squeezed his hand back as if to say, *You're welcome.*

* * * * *

Inez had waited while the Mass made the changes to its Hunters, the time passing for her in an almost dreamlike fashion. When the process was complete, she returned to full awareness. It wasn't like waking from sleep. One moment she was detached, mind empty, and the next she was awake and alert, as if she were a computer that had gone into rest mode until its user needed it again. She supposed in a very real sense, that's what she was now. This thought didn't distress her. This was her new reality, and she accepted it. Besides, she was far more interested in field testing the new improved Hunters.

Let's do it, she thought.

* * * * *

Lee Fleming had lived in Bridgewater all her life, and she'd never desired to go anywhere else, even after Janae had torn the place all to hell. Her daddy had started Big-Time Tow, and while the business might never have lived up to its name, it had put food on the table. Dominic Fleming had towed broken-down vehicles for twenty-two years before his heart decided it had had enough of this world and quit on him. Lee had been nineteen at the time and working as a cashier at Burnt Pig Barbecue when she decided to continue her daddy's legacy. She was twenty-eight now, and while the towing business wasn't exactly glamorous, it suited her well enough.

She liked her gig with the movie people. They needed her to move their monster around for them, and while that was fun, what she liked most was seeing that cute special effects guy. The monster didn't go anywhere without him, and he always rode in the cab with her whenever the monster needed to travel. She had always been comfortable talking to people, and she'd struck up a conversation with Enrique the first time she'd met him, and they'd spoken more each time she'd hauled the monster to one place or another. Besides being cute, he was easy to talk to and genuinely seemed like a nice guy, and she'd decided she'd ask him out for a drink tonight. She figured there was a good chance he'd say yes. And after that, who knew? Maybe they'd both get lucky.

She was short and on the curvy side, and while she might not look like a cover girl, she had no trouble finding guys to date. As far as she was concerned, being sexy was mostly about self-confidence, and she had plenty of that. She wore a white tank top, jeans, and sneakers. The jeans were tight and the top displayed a good amount of cleavage – maybe too much – but she liked Enrique, so what the hell?

The sun had only begun to dip below the horizon when she pulled up to the beach. She was early – Enrique had said to come back at dusk – but she'd been too eager to see him to wait any longer. She knew she'd risk interrupting filming by coming early, but so what? Didn't movie directors do a lot of takes?

She drove slowly onto the sand. Her vehicle had four-wheel drive, but she wanted to avoid getting stuck if she could. How embarrassing would that be? Her, a local girl, not knowing how to drive on the beach?

She didn't see anyone, but that wasn't too surprising. The sheriff had closed this section of the beach so the movie folks could film. There were signs posted on the street next to the beach, and there were barriers – a pair of broom handles stuck into the sand with yellow caution tape stretched between them – at each end of the reserved sections. People gathered to watch the filming and take pictures on the sly, but so far as she knew, no one had snuck into the restricted area. But there was no sign of the cast and crew, either, which struck her as odd. From what Enrique had told her, their producer was a slave driver who kept them working every moment she could. Maybe they'd finished today's beach scenes and were filming elsewhere. If so, she hoped Enrique had remained with the mechanical pliosaur. She didn't see him next to the monster, though. Maybe he was on the other side of it? She sounded her horn a couple times, but he didn't appear.

Shit. Well, she knew he'd return to the beach when the sun went down. No way he'd let her tow Bob without him. She'd just have to wait.

She pulled her truck up to where Bob rested off shore, maneuvered the vehicle until the rear faced the dinosaur, then turned off the engine. She briefly considered sitting and listening to the radio, but as she'd approached she'd seen a new prop lying on the beach – a wounded shark – which she assumed Enrique had made, and she wanted to get a look at it. That way, she'd have something new to talk to him about when she saw him.

She climbed out of the truck – leaving the keys in the ignition – shut the door and started walking toward the shark. On the way, she noticed Bob's head was tilted at a weird angle. Had the dinosaur gotten damaged during filming? If so, Enrique would probably be too busy fixing it to go out with her tonight. Maybe she could keep him company while he worked? And if they took a few breaks to "get to know each other better," what was the harm in that?

She knew something was wrong before she reached the shark. For one thing, it looked *too* real. Its head was nothing but ragged, blood-soaked meat and cartilage, and while she knew special effects artists could work wonders, Enrique had told her that he only had a small budget to work with, and most of that money had been spent on Bob. But as good as the dinosaur was, it still looked like an overgrown toy. But this shark looked – and more disgustingly, smelled – like the real deal. She smelled blood combined with a fishy odor and the scent of incipient rot. She wasn't sure what kind of shark it was. Just because she'd grown up next to the ocean didn't mean she was an expert in marine biology. But she'd never seen one with red veins running through its skin like this. It was that detail which made her reconsider her original thought. Maybe this was a special effect. But then she realized there was no reason for Enrique to make it smell like an actual dead shark. No, the thing was real, but what the hell was it doing here and what had happened to it?

Had it got its head caught in a boat propeller, died, and then washed up on the beach, probably after filming was done for the day? That seemed the likeliest explanation. And maybe those red veins were some kind of injury too, although she felt less confident about this theory.

She felt a prickle on the back of her neck then, as if someone was watching her. But when she looked around, she saw nothing.

Maybe it *would* be a good idea to wait for Enrique in the truck. But before she could start back toward her vehicle, a wave rolled into shore, and when it receded, it left something behind. Something that looked very much like Enrique's head. The grisly thing lay on its right side, eyes wide, mouth open. It had what looked like teeth marks on its forehead, and its neck was a ragged stump. Part of her hoped this was some kind of fucked-up practical joke, that Enrique had made a replica of his head and left it here to scare her. If so, it would be a complete dick move, and no way in hell would she go out with him then, but it would be far better than the alternative – that this was real and Enrique was dead.

And then she saw the fins break the surface – many, many fins – and they were all heading for the beach. She saw the crimson veins on the fins, and she had the crazy thought that these were the headless shark's friends coming to avenge their dead comrade. She felt a cold tightness in her gut upon seeing so many sharks advancing toward her, and she took a step back, ready to make a dash for the truck. But then she stopped herself. She might not be a marine biologist, but it didn't take a degree to know that sharks were only dangerous in the water. They might look scary, but so long as she remained standing where she was, they couldn't hurt her. She continued watching, feeling a bit better now. She assumed they would slow as they drew closer to shore and the water became shallower. She figured they'd break off and head back out to sea or start swimming in circles offshore. But before either of these things happened, she wanted to get a picture. Otherwise, who'd believe her when she told this story?

She carried her phone in her back pocket, and she quickly pulled it out, opened the photo app, and held the device in front of her face. On the screen, she saw a smaller image of the crimson-threaded shark fins coming toward her. She tapped the screen to focus the camera and then began taking pictures. She took one shot after another, as fast as she could, but as she did, she realized something that caused her stomach to roil with nausea. The sharks weren't stopping.

As the first ones came onto shore, she thought they'd beached themselves, but they kept moving forward, undulating like insects. Their bodies – seven, maybe eight feet long – were covered by those strange red veins, and their eyes were the same red. Weird pink frond-like growths extended from their gills, pulsing as they came. They glided across the sand, trailing red umbilical cords that were attached to their bodies behind their dorsal fins. At first, she had no idea how the sharks managed to move on the shore, and then she saw their undersides were covered by tiny hair-like structures, thousands of them, that functioned like miniature legs. A word that she hadn't heard since high school biology class popped into her head: *cilia*.

What she was seeing wasn't real, *couldn't* be real. It had to be some kind of elaborate special effect. The movie people were filming a scene, and she'd wandered onto a live set without realizing it. So what if no one else was around, if there were no signs of any actors or crew members, if Enrique wasn't here to supervise the effects? (Because his head was lying on the wet sand.) Since it was impossible for this nightmarish scene to be real, it was fake, which meant it was part of the movie. End of discussion.

So she stood and watched as more and more sharks crawled out of the water and onto the sand. Although she was fairly certain sharks didn't make any sounds, she expected these creatures to growl and snarl as they came. Didn't the shark in *Jaws IV* roar in that movie? But these creatures were silent, save for the soft scuttling sounds made by their cilia-like legs.

She didn't know what broke her paralysis. Maybe something about these monstrous sharks finally convinced her they were real. Or maybe her mind simply decided she couldn't afford to take any chances. Whatever the case, she turned and ran toward her truck. The sand gave beneath her feet, slowing her down, but it didn't have the same effect on the sharks. The first one to reach her managed to snag hold of her left sneaker, bringing her down. She fell onto the sand, the impact driving the air from her lungs. But she didn't get a chance to catch her breath again. Sharks fell upon her like a pack of starving dogs and tore her apart within seconds. She died so fast that she didn't even have time for a final thought.

Several of the sharks carried the largest chunks of her body back toward the ocean, intending to deliver them to the Mass. The rest of the sharks continued moving up the beach, heading toward Bridgewater, umbilical cords lengthening as they went.

* * * * *

Inez was pleased by the successful test run. Now it was time for the main show to start.

Lights . . . camera . . . action!

CHAPTER SEVEN

Boyd Campbell had wanted to be a screenwriter for as long as he could remember. The first time he became aware that there were people behind the movies he watched was when he was eight. Normally, he paid no attention to the names that appeared on the screen before and after a movie, but for some reason this time he did. He was sitting on the living room couch while his mom was in the kitchen making lunch, and when he saw a person's name appear on the screen beneath the words *Written By*, he got up and walked into the kitchen. His mother was mixing tuna salad in a plastic bowl with a long wooden spoon, and when she noticed Boyd standing behind her, she stopped mixing and turned to look at him.

"I want to write a movie," he said.

She didn't laugh at him, didn't tell him he was too young to do such a thing. Instead, she smiled and said, "That sounds like fun."

After that day, he put on his own "movies" using action figures to perform the parts he'd created. When he reached middle school, he wrote and directed short videos he made with friends. After graduating high school, he moved to California and studied film at UCLA, eventually going on to get an MFA in Film and Television Production. When he graduated, he imagined himself writing films that mattered, that changed the way people viewed cinema, themselves, and their culture. So why was he now sitting cross-legged on a bed in a moldy hotel room, laptop open before him, reworking a shitty script about sea monsters?

His scripts had been good enough to land him an agent, and when she contacted him to say that Imagitopia was interested in his work, he was guardedly optimistic. Imagitopia was a small studio, so it had some indie cred, but the films it produced weren't exactly works of art. Inze brought him in for a meeting, and while she said she liked his scripts, she had a specific project in mind that she'd like him to write a script for. He'd since learned that Inez liked working with young screenwriters because they were cheap and usually so desperate to get a start in the industry they pretty much did whatever she told them.

When she told him about her idea for *Devourer from the Deep*, he'd wanted no part of it. But then she started telling him about her true intentions for the film. Under the guise of a simple monster movie, she wanted to tell a story about how modern humans had lost touch with the past, and indeed, the very planet they lived on. The monster in the film – a pliosaur – would be a symbol of that disconnection. And the pliosaur wasn't merely an imaginary monster. Dozens of the damn things had been discovered in the ocean off the western coast of South America. Because of this link to reality, the movie's themes would hit audiences harder.

By the time the meeting was over, Boyd was convinced Inez wanted him to write a metafictional postmodern take on B-movie monsters as metaphors for the human race's stubborn refusal to accept they were killing themselves by the way they treated their environment. Plus, he'd get credit as sole writer on the film. Inez sent a contract to his agent, she reviewed it, told Boyd that it wasn't great, but what more could he expect as a new writer, and he signed it. And now he was on location in Texas, trying to figure out how to write monster attack scenes when they didn't have a functioning monster to film with. Not exactly how he pictured his first Hollywood gig would go.

He'd written precisely ten words since Inez had sent him off to do yet another revision on the script – which at this point bore little resemblance to the first draft he'd written – and of these words, he'd deleted eight. And he was thinking about cutting the other two as well.

"Shit!"

He closed his laptop and got off the bed. It was going to be a long night, and if he hoped to finish the revisions by morning, he needed some serious caffeine. The Sea Breeze provided in-room coffeemakers, but the staff only left a couple prepackaged filters every day, and he'd already used those. Plus, the water from the sink he'd used to make the coffee made it taste musty. Instead of going to the front desk to ask for more filters, he thought he'd go down to the small coffee joint located a few blocks from here, in an entertainment district called Sailor's Walk. It wasn't Starbucks, but the coffee was a hell of a lot better than what he could get here. He'd take his laptop, sit at a table, and drink coffee until the place closed. Plus, on the way there, he'd pass by a number of buildings that had been damaged by Hurricane Janae and abandoned. He found the sad, empty structures inspirational – symbols of loss given three-dimensional life. He might even incorporate them into a future script someday.

He put on his shoes, grabbed his room key, and then picked up his computer and tucked it beneath his arm. He knew a big part of the reason he was relocating was so he could put off getting to work a little longer, and he was fine with that. He'd had a professor in college who'd said procrastination was a writer's middle name. Boyd wholeheartedly agreed.

His room faced the ocean, and the light of the setting sun colored the water molten orange. Normally, he would've been struck by the beauty of the sight, might've pondered using the image in a script, maybe as an opening shot. But he barely noticed the ocean because his gaze was fixed on the creatures emerging from its water. The beach was covered by sharks that seemed to be swimming across the sand. The sight of these things – which also had strange growths protruding from their gills and long umbilical cords attached to their bodies – was so startling that for a moment all Boyd could do was stare at them.

The sharks headed inland, a number of them coming toward the Sea Breeze. As the first of them drew close, Boyd saw the red veins beneath their skin, saw their blood-filled eyes, and he thought *If I put these things in a script, no one would take them seriously.*

The section of the beach closest to the hotel had been reserved for filming, so it was empty, except for the mechanical pliosaur and a tow truck. The hotel wasn't empty, though, and as the sharks approached, several people stepped out of the rooms to gaze upon the absurd and nightmarish scene spread out before them. One of these people was a middle-aged man who worked the front desk. He took one look at the sharks trundling toward the hotel and said, "What in the holy jumping Jesus *are* those things?" And then a shark leaped toward him, angling its head as it did so, and caught hold of his torso in its jaws. The man tried to scream as the shark bore him to the ground, but the only thing to emerge from his mouth was a gurgling fountain of blood.

The hotel clerk going down made everyone realize that regardless of how crazy this situation was, these sharks were real, and they could kill. People screamed. Some ran back into their rooms and shut their doors, while others – spurred by panic – fled. Sharks brought down the latter in short order and leaped through windows, shattering glass, in their attempts to get at the former.

Boyd stood in front of his room's closed door, unsure what to do. This seemed to be a classic case of damned if you do, damned if you don't. An excellent dilemma to put a movie hero into, but a truly shitty situation for a real person. He only had seconds to make a choice, and since it was obvious he couldn't outrun these things, that meant he really didn't have a choice, did he? He pulled his key from his pocket – dropping his laptop in the process – and opened the door. He ran inside, laptop forgotten, and slammed the door shut a split second before one of the sharks collided with it. Out of reflex, Boyd engaged the door chair – like *that* was going to help – and hurried toward the bathroom. He was halfway there when the window exploded inward and a shark flew into the room. The creature hit the floor then crawled up onto the bed, giving Boyd a glimpse at the hundreds of tiny legs protruding from its underside.

What the actual fuck?

He ran to the bathroom, shut the door, and threw his weight against it, bracing it. The shark struck the door, but this one wasn't as sturdy as the room's outer door, and Boyd felt it bow inward with the horrible sound of cracking wood. He thought the frame had been damaged, but the door held. For now.

The shark struck it again and again, and each time the frame broke a little more. Boyd had the strange feeling that the shark was purposely toying with him. As big as the damn thing was, it should've had no trouble breaking in. A single blow should've been sufficient. So why draw it out? The answer that came to him was insane, but it felt right.

To make it more suspenseful.

There was a pause, and Boyd allowed himself to hope the shark had given up, either to go in search of easier prey or because despite its weird gills, it could only remain out of water for so long and had to return. But then it slammed into the door again – much harder this time – and the door burst inward, tearing free from its hinges and falling onto Boyd. The shark crawled onto the door, and its weight pressed Boyd down to the tiled floor. As he lay there, he realized that he'd gotten the attack scenes in *Devourer from the Deep* all wrong. When he'd written about people getting eaten by the pliosaur in the script, he'd described them as *filled with terror* and *on the verge of losing their sanity*. But the reality was far different, at least for him. He was scared, sure, but most of all, he was pissed off. Not only was he going to die before his first film was released, he was going to be killed by a monster even more ridiculous than the one he'd written about. One good thing about dying, though: at least he wouldn't have to pay off the rest of his student loans.

He closed his eyes, gritted his teeth, and waited for the shark to find a way to get under the door and begin tearing at his flesh.

But that didn't happen.

After a moment, he heard the shark scuttle backward, and he felt its weight lift. He waited several more moments, fearing the shark had retreated only to prepare to attack once more. But when it didn't, he pushed the bathroom door off of him, slid out from under it, and stood.

There were two sharks in his bedroom now. The closest he presumed had been the one that had battered down the bathroom door. The other stood on the bed, it too having come in through the broken window, Boyd figured. This second shark held something in its mouth, and it wasn't until the creature dropped it did Boyd realize it was his laptop. The sharks looked at him for a moment, and although their faces were incapable of expression and their eyes remained an unchanging red, he had the strangest sensation the animals were trying to communicate with him somehow. Then the second shark bent its head toward his laptop and nudged it.

Boyd frowned.

"You want me to . . . write?"

Neither shark responded to his words. They regarded him a moment longer before moving backward across the floor and through the broken window.

Easier to keep their cords from getting tangled that way, he thought.

And then they were gone.

Boyd didn't move for a long time. When he finally worked up the courage, he walked to the broken window and looked outside. The sun was down now, but it still wasn't completely dark, and he could see dozens of umbilical cords stretching from the water, across the beach, and into town.

"That's not good," Boyd said. But he couldn't help thinking that what had just happened would make a hell of an opening scene.

* * * * *

Tamara lay atop a blanket spread out on the floor of what had once been a small saltwater taffy shop. She was naked, her legs lifted high in the air. Shari Dawson – equally naked – pressed her face against Tamara's vagina, her tongue working its magic. Tamara gripped Shari's hair and every once in a while, she gave it a hard tug, and Shari would moan and laugh. Tamara wondered if Shari could taste the residue of her husband's cum inside her. If she did, would it turn her on or would she be pissed to learn Tamara had been fucking Pete? Tamara briefly considered telling her about Pete right then to see how she would react, but she decided against it. Why spoil the woman's fun? Or hers, for that matter?

Tamara flirted with pretty much everyone she met. Most of the time, she did so unconsciously, and she managed to attract a great many lovers this way. Shari had been one of those cases. Tamara had had lunch with Shari at an Italian place in Sailor's Walk the first day they'd started filming. Shari had said that getting to know Tamara would help her better portray her when she filled in during action scenes. The sexual energy between them was immediate and strong, and before lunch was over, they'd finger banged each other in a restroom stall. Unlike her husband – who Tamara seduced the next day – Shari liked to have sex in public areas. She said she enjoyed the risk factor, and that was fine with Tamara. Not only because it was exciting, but because this way she didn't have to worry about Pete and Shari accidentally running into each other at her hotel room.

For their rendezvous this evening, Tamara had chosen an abandoned shop across the street from Flotsam, where most of the cast and crew – Pete included – had gathered to drink and shoot the shit. Tamara had picked out the place earlier, broken the glass on the door so she could reach in and unlock it, lay the blanket on the floor, then closed the door and returned to the set. Now she was here and building to her third orgasm of the evening and enjoying herself immensely.

As much fun as Pete and Shari were separately, Tamara thought the sex would be even better if the three of them all got together at the same time. She wasn't sure how to bring up the topic, though, since neither Pete nor Shari knew Tamara was fucking them both. She could be pretty damn persuasive when she wanted to, and while Pete and Shari might be angry with each other when they learned the truth, Tamara thought she'd be able to bring them around eventually. After all, they wouldn't be the first couple she'd convinced to join her in a little group action. She decided to bring up the subject of a threesome to Shari – *without* mentioning she'd been fucking her husband – to gauge Shari's response to the idea. *After* she came again, of course. But just as she was on the verge of climaxing, she heard a scream coming from somewhere out on the street.

Shari raised her head and said, "What was that?"

Tamara's almost-orgasm began to fizzle, but before she could get hold of Shari's head and push her back down to her crotch, there came another scream, this one louder and closer.

Tamara sat up. What the fuck was going on? Sailor's Walk had once been a thriving entertainment district before Janae, and while half of the establishments were closed, the buildings vacated and boarded up, the other half were still open, and if they didn't pack in the customers these days, they did enough business to survive. Sailor's Walk wasn't exactly a lawless urban wasteland teeming with murderers and rapists. But that scream sure sounded like someone was in trouble. *Bad* trouble.

Tamara didn't bother grabbing her clothes or even covering herself with the blanket as she walked towards the taffy shop's grime-streaked window. She wasn't afraid of being seen by anyone outside. There was no light in the shop, and she wasn't self-conscious about her body in the slightest. She looked fantastic naked, and she knew it. Shari followed, remaining behind Tamara, obviously less comfortable with the idea of standing nude at a window.

The streetlights had been fashioned to resemble old-fashioned lamp poles, only with electric bulbs instead of flames. The illumination they provided was dim, an attempt to create a classy-cozy atmosphere, Tamara thought. But right now, she'd have preferred the bright garish glow of fluorescent lights so they could better see what the fuck was going on. The streets of Sailor's Walk were covered with cobblestones and closed to vehicular traffic, an affectation Tamara thought designed to give the area the feeling of an old New England coastal town, but which came off as an inferior – and more than a little sad – imitation.

"Do you see anything?" Shari asked. She'd placed her hands on Tamara's shoulders and her fingers dug into the skin. Tamara was surprised by Shari's fear. She would've expected a big, bad stuntwoman to have bigger balls. Tamara was scared, too, but when she got frightened, it was all fight with her and no flight.

She put her hands up to shield her eyes and pressed close to the window, smooshing her breasts against the glass. *Anyone who walks by right now will get a hell of show,* she thought.

She didn't see anything, and after several moments she was ready to give up. But just as she was about to draw back, a man stumbled forward and smacked into the window. Shari let out a small scream of her own, and her fingers dug into Tamara's shoulders with enough force to draw blood. Tamara tried to pull back from the window, but Shari held her in place, so all she could do was look at the man, whose forehead touched the glass a foot above where her tits were pressed. He showed no interest – or indeed, any awareness – that she was naked, and Tamara might have been insulted if the man's face and clothes hadn't been covered in blood. Blood she thought was due to the ragged stump where his right arm had been. He had a hell of a good reason to be preoccupied.

He was a young man, in his early twenties, Tamara guessed, with glasses, a small goatee, and black stubble on his shaved head. He wore a light gray T-shirt – which was now splotched with crimson – khaki cargo shorts, and sandals. His eyes found Tamara's, and she saw pain, confusion, and desperation in his gaze. He opened and closed his mouth several times as if he were trying to speak, but no sound emerged, and she was unable to read his lips.

"Let go of me, Shari," she said, wriggling to try to dislodge the other woman. "That guy needs help!"

But before Tamara could get free, something large and black slammed into the man and bore him down to the sidewalk. The man released a high-pitched shriek so horrible that Tamara actually peed a little. Shari's fingers still dug into her flesh, and the woman was pressed so hard against her back that it felt as if they'd been sealed together by industrial strength epoxy. But Tamara might not have retreated from the window even if she could. Her curiosity was simply too strong to deny. She looked down at the sidewalk and saw what appeared to be a motherfucking shark chewing the shit out of the guy. The shark had torn open the man's abdomen and was now pulling out coils of intestine and gulping them down. Despite this horrendous injury, the man still lived, and he screamed and thrashed as the shark – a goddamned *shark* – feasted. Tamara noted the strange additions to the shark's anatomy, red eyes, veiny hide, weird frills, and the cord attached to its back, but none was as bizarre as seeing a fish kill someone on dry land.

"What is it?"

Shari's face was pressed between Tamara's shoulder blades, and thus the woman couldn't see what was happening outside. *Lucky her,* Tamara thought.

"I'm not sure," Tamara said, her voice shaky but clear. "It looks like the guy's being eaten by some kind of . . . something." She couldn't bring herself to say the word *shark*. The idea was too ludicrous to speak aloud.

There was more shouting and screaming, and an instant later a group of people came running down the street. Tamara didn't know where they'd come from – a bar or restaurant farther down the street, probably – but they looked terrified. A second later, Tamara saw why. Three more of the impossible sharks pursued them, the creatures gliding across the cobblestones with strange undulating motions, moving as swiftly as if they were still in the water. The sharks quickly caught up with the people at the tail end of the crowd, and they lost no time in bringing them down and chomping away. Blood sprayed the air, and the victims screamed as they died. The sharks did something curious then. Instead of eating their prey, they abandoned them and went off in pursuit of those who were still running, as if the creatures were determined none of them would get away. The shark outside the taffy shop's window did the same, leaving the ravaged body of the guy with the stubble head to join in pursuit of the runners. Once the last shark was gone, all that remained in the street were several dead bodies and four stretched-out umbilical cords.

Tamara realized then that she wasn't the sole witness to what had happened. Across the street, the Flotsam's door was cracked open, and the owner – Susan – was peering out. Tamara made a decision. She reached up, pulled Shari's hands off her shoulders, which stung like hell from where Shari's nails had cut into her flesh, and took hold of one of her hands.

"Come on. We need to get across the street before more of those things show up."

"What things?" Shari asked, but Tamara knew this wasn't a time for explanations. Pulling Shari along after her, she headed for the taffy shop's front door. She'd left it unlocked and she opened it now and dragged Shari out onto the sidewalk with her.

"Don't close the door!" Tamara shouted at Susan. "We're coming over!"

Susan opened the bar's door wider, and her face registered surprise when she saw Tamara and Shari were both naked. Tamara pulled Shari into the street, and they both slipped in blood that had spilled from Stubble-Head's ravaged gut. They managed not to fall, but only because they had each other to steady themselves. Stubble-head amazingly still clung to life, and he rolled over, spilling more of his intestines onto the ground, and reached out to them with his one remaining hand. Tamara thought he might've whispered, "Help me," but it might've been nothing but a final wordless gust of air from his dying lungs. Then the man fell still, eyes remaining open, lips parted in a soundless eternal sigh.

When Shari saw Stubble-Head and the other dead men and women lying in the street, she let out a choked sob. Tamara would've told her to close her eyes as they crossed the street, but they needed to make sure they didn't trip on the land sharks' umbilical cords, and Shari would need to keep her eyes open for that. The umbilical cords were *disgusting*. They pulsed and quivered hideously, and they stank like rotten fish and seaweed.

The cobblestones hurt like hell on Tamara's bare feet, and when the two women were halfway across the street, she heard a *whhsk-whhsk-whhsk* sound, like thousands of tiny bristles moving across the cobblestones. She looked to her left and saw another pair of sharks gliding toward them, mouths open and red eyes blazing.

"Fuck!" Tamara shouted, and she started running, yanking Shari along behind her. Shari screamed when she saw the sharks, and while Tamara knew how she felt, she didn't want to waste any breath right then. She needed it all for running. She could've run faster if she hadn't been pulling Shari along behind her, and there was a moment – an infinitesimally small moment – when she considered letting the woman go. A punch line from a joke flashed through her mind then. *I don't have to outrun the bear. I just have to outrun you.* She didn't do it, of course. She wasn't in love with Shari. For Christ's sake, she'd only known the woman for a few days – but Tamara, vain and self-centered as she might be, wasn't a piece of shit human being.

Susan threw the door open wide as they approached and stepped aside so the two women could run past her. Then she slammed the door shut and engaged the locks. Half the people in the bar were standing, probably having responded to the screams of the sharks' victims. The other half were still seated, perhaps undecided about what, if anything, they should do. But now all of them stared at Tamara and Shari, minds struggling to process why the hell the two of them were naked.

Unsurprisingly, it was Pete who spoke first.

"Are you two . . . uh . . . all right?"

He sounded both scared and angry, and Tamara decided she didn't have time to deal with his hurt feelings.

"Pete, Shari – I've been fucking both of you. We can worry about that later, though because –"

Something large and heavy slammed into the bar's front window, causing cracks to spiderweb across its surface.

"– a bunch of fucked-up landsharks are attacking the town," she finished.

The window broke and glass shards flew into the bar, followed by the creatures Tamara had spoken of. And then the screaming started.

CHAPTER EIGHT

Boyd trailed the sharks to Sailor's Walk. It wasn't difficult. All he had to do was follow their umbilical cords. Once, he'd paused to bend down and touch one, and had been surprised to find it warm. The flesh gave beneath his fingers a little, but it felt tough, almost leathery. It had taken him some minutes after the two sharks had broken into his hotel room to work up the courage to venture outside, but he had, and while several other sharks had passed him, none paid him any attention. It seemed he was immune from attack – at least for now.

The sharks made straight for Sailor's Walk, as if they knew they'd find the greatest concentration of victims there, at least this close to the beach from where they'd emerged. It was weird how they seemed to operate as a unified group, almost as if they possessed an intelligence of some kind. He remembered how the one shark had brought his laptop back into the room and given it a nudge, as if to tell him to get back to work, and he shuddered. Dumb monsters were bad enough, but smart ones were way worse.

As he walked, he passed the remains of men and women who hadn't managed to escape the sharks. The bodies had been savagely torn apart, but as near as he could tell, the sharks had eaten little of their prey. But then, these weren't regular sharks, were they? For all that people feared sharks, in the end they were just animals, doing what they did in order to survive and perpetuate their species. They didn't attack to inflict pain or for the thrill of the kill. Humans did those things. But *these* creatures, these . . . *demon sharks* were different. They appeared to kill indiscriminately and for no apparent reason. No, not completely indiscriminately. They wouldn't kill *him*. Boyd wasn't sure why, but he was beginning to have the sneaking suspicion that he had been spared to witness the sharks' attack on Bridgewater so he could write about it later and tell the world of the monsters' bloodthirsty might. *That* was the message the demon shark had given him when it had returned his laptop. The notion seemed insane, but it felt right to him, so it would do until another hypothesis presented itself. Or he got eaten, whichever came first.

As he walked down the street, being careful to avoid stepping on any body parts or umbilical cords, he felt strangely disconnected from himself, as if he were simultaneously a character in a movie and an audience member watching himself.

I suppose I'm in shock.

He made a mental note to remember this sensation so he could write about it later.

Without realizing he'd done so, he'd headed in the direction of Flotsam, and now the bar was in sight. Sharks were clustered around the establishment, and more were coming, as if responding to a silent call. The creatures crawled over one another as they fought to get through the broken window. It was the same tactic the sharks that had entered his hotel room had used, only on a larger scale.

If something works, you stick with it.

It took him a moment to remember that Flotsam was where the *Devourer*'s cast and crew hung out after work. This meant that his co-workers – he couldn't really call any of them friends – were under attack. Some of them might already be dead. He supposed he should take a look. After all, it seemed his role in this madness was to bear witness, so he might as well get on with it.

He walked around the writhing mass of demon sharks, went to Flotsam's front door, opened it, and stepped inside.

* * * * *

Tasha grimaced as the first of the sharks came in through the broken window. As hideous as the things were, she grimaced not out of revulsion, but from pain. Her head was filled with crackling static, like a radio that couldn't pick up a station, only turned up to deafening volume. It felt as if someone had shoved a white-hot blade through the middle of her brain. Her entire body went limp, and she would've fallen off her chair if Jarrod hadn't grabbed hold of her arm and lifted her to her feet as he stood. Bonnie screamed, jumped to her feet, and grabbed hold of Jarrod's other arm.

Chaos erupted in the bar.

The sharks – or whatever the hell they were – began tearing into the people closest to them. The first to go down were some of the locals that had been working on the movie, as well as Tony and Nina. A shark tore off Tony's right arm, and a second ripped off his left leg. He went down then, and another shark took off his head. Nina screamed as Tony's blood splattered her face and chest, and then the shark that had taken Tony's arm spat it out and rushed toward her. It rammed her in the stomach, the impact breaking her spine. The instant she fell to the floor, the shark tore into her battered abdomen and began feasting on the soft, sweet treats within.

Tasha concentrated on muting the static jangling in her head, but the most she was able to do was lower the volume to a tolerable level. It still hurt, but at least she was no longer in danger of passing out.

As the sharks killed their first victims, Pete yanked the rusty machete from the wall and moved in front of both Shari and Tamara, as if to protect them. Tasha had known about the couple's separate affairs with Tamara, but she was still surprised to see Pete ready to defend them both. Maybe he wasn't quite the selfish asshole she'd pegged him as. Susan rushed back behind the bar, ducked down, came up with a pump-action shotgun in her hands, and began firing without hesitation. Everyone else tried to run, with varying degrees of success.

Saul – despite not having the most athletic build – hauled ass toward the back of the bar like he was an Olympic-level sprinter. Tasha knew the restrooms were back there, but was there a back door? She supposed Saul would find out soon.

Tasha didn't know how much training or experience Susan had with a gun, but a half dozen sharks had made their way into the bar, and still more were fighting to get in. The damn things were so big that it would've been shocking if Susan missed hitting any of them. Tasha half expected the rounds to bound off the monsters' hides, but the pellets tore into the creatures with small explosions of blood. The wounds didn't seem to slow them down any, but she could sense the reaction of their nervous systems to the injuries, and she felt confident they could be killed.

Besides their strange eyes, skin veins, gill growths, and centipede-like legs on their undersides, the sharks had fleshy tubes a couple inches in diameter attached to their backs and trailing out the windows. What were those things? Were they like the oxygen lines deep-sea divers used, only in reverse? Did they pump saltwater into the sharks to help them survive on land? She reached her mind out toward one of the sharks, and the static in her head grew louder again. Yes, the tubes were for water, but they also connected the sharks to a larger mind, one that was controlling them. She recognized it as the presence she'd sensed earlier on the beach, only now there was something different about it. Different, yet at the same time familiar. It was confusing, but she thought if she could psychically follow one of the tubes back to its source, she might be able to connect with the boss' mind, and –

A round from Susan's shotgun struck the tube of the shark Tasha had been focusing on, and reddish-pink fluid gushed out of the resulting tear. The shark – which had been chewing a man's groin to bloody mush – arched its back, raised its head, and roared with pain. No, that wasn't right. The creature made no actual sound, but Tasha heard its agony in her mind as if it *were* sound. The shark began thrashing back and forth, its entire body quivering, as if it was having a stroke or something. The tube grew taut, and then it pulled loose from the shark in a spray of blood. Tasha got a brief glimpse of the barbed end of the tube before it flew back through the window and was gone. As soon as the tube retracted, the shark shuddered from snout to tail, collapsed to the floor, and lay still.

Things had continued to happen while Tasha had been focused on the dying shark. Susan had run out of ammo, and she had run from behind the bar and was heading in the direction Saul had taken.

"Follow me!" she shouted.

"Never let it be said that I didn't know how to take direction," Jarrod said. Holding onto both Tasha and Bonnie's hands, he followed after Susan, pulling the other two women along with him.

Tasha cast her awareness around the bar one last time, searching for any survivors. Why, she wasn't sure. It wasn't as if she could do anything to help them. She sensed only dead or nearly dead minds, but then she found one that was still conscious. Even though her eyes were pointed toward the rear of the bar as Jarrod hustled her and Bonnie along, she could still see the woman's face in her mind. It was Tina. The soundwoman had been eviscerated, yet her lungs and heart continued to function weakly. She lay on the wooden floor, blood pooled all around her. Some of it hers, most of it not. She gazed up at the ceiling, knowing that she was going to die, that it was only a matter of moments before her heart finally realized the body it was housed in was dead and stopped beating. But one of the sharks didn't intend to let her die peacefully. As the rest of its companions raced after the fleeing humans, it crawled onto Tina. She was too weak to feel its insect legs and heavy weight on what remained of her body. Her vision had become blurry around the edges, but she could still see well enough. Tasha didn't know if the shark was aware of this – didn't see how the animal could be – but it lowered its head so Tina could see its mouth and then displayed double rows of triangular white teeth. This wasn't the act of a predator preparing to feed. It was instead an act of deliberate cruelty, something only a human mind was capable of.

After a long moment, the shark lunged toward Tina's face. Moving with the speed of thought, Tasha reached into Tina's memories and pulled out one of the woman's favorites: the day when her father surprised her by bringing home a golden retriever puppy. It was this image – along with the emotions that accompanied it – that followed Tina down into death.

It seemed Tasha had been able to do something for Tina after all. She only wished she could've done more.

And then Jarrod was pushing her ahead of him up a narrow flight of stairs behind Susan, and she ran upward, not knowing where they were going and – for the moment – not caring. It was enough to still be alive.

* * * * *

Jarrod had no idea where Susan was leading them, and he didn't give a rat's hairy ass, just so long as it was away from those shark-things. There was a door at the top of the stairs, and Susan opened it and hurried through. She held the door for the rest of them, and they rushed past her and into what Jarrod assumed were her living quarters. Couch, coffee table, end tables, a couple of floor lamps, a Persian rug . . . The most interesting item was a framed photo of an exhausted but determined long-distance runner on one wall. There was a kitchenette at one end of the room, and past that a small hallway which Jarrod presumed led to a bathroom and bedroom.

As soon as everyone was inside, Susan slammed the door shut and locked it. Then without a word, she ran to the kitchenette, opened a drawer, and pulled out a box of shells. She put them on the counter and began reloading her gun. Jarrod nodded in approval. This was a woman who would have a good chance of being the last person standing if this was a horror film.

Jarrod had been too busy running to keep track of who else had escaped the sharks, but he took stock now. Aside from him and Susan, there was Tasha and Bonnie, Pete, Shari, and Tamara – the latter two still as naked as the day they were born. And . . . that was it. When they'd been running up the stairs, it had seemed like there were twice as many at least. But there were only six of them. So few compared to how many people had been in the bar.

Saul wasn't here, and Jarrod thought the director had been killed along with the others, but then he remembered seeing Saul jump up from his seat when the attack began and haul ass toward the restrooms. He hoped there was a rear exit back there and that Saul had made it out. He didn't consider Saul a coward who'd deserted them. He just had quicker reflexes than the rest of them, that's all. He hoped Saul was still alive, but if there were more of those things outside the back of the building . . .

"Go in my bedroom and get some clothes," Susan said. She didn't look up from reloading as she spoke, and neither did she say who she was addressing, but since there were only two naked people present, it wasn't any great mystery who her words were intended for.

Tamara took hold of Shari's hand and pulled her down the hallway. Shari glanced back at Pete, and it looked as if he was going to say something, but he must've thought better of it because he remained silent. He still held the rusty machete, and now he examined it closely.

"You got a knife sharpener, Susan?" he asked.

77

Susan reached into another drawer, pulled out a small knife sharpner, and tossed it on the counter. Pete joined her in the kitchenette and began sharpening the machete's blade.

"It's like the opposite of a horror film," Tamara said, almost smiling. "Everyone's doing the right things."

"So far," Jarrod said.

"What the hell *are* those fucking things?" Bonnie asked. She spoke loud and fast, her voice on the edge of hysteria.

"More importantly, what if they follow us up the stairs?" Pete said.

Jarrod wanted to tell Pete not to be ridiculous. Whoever heard of sharks climbing stairs? But then who'd ever heard of sharks crashing through the window of a bar on dry land? He rather felt a bit hysterical himself, but he should know what to do, shouldn't he? After all, his entire career had prepared him for a scenario like this. But now that it was here, he didn't have the first idea what to do.

"We need to find a way out of the building," Tasha said. "A *safe* way."

"I'm not sure any way is safe right now," Jarrod said. "But I take your point." Once again, he had the strange sense that Tasha had known what he'd been thinking. But she was right. They needed to get out of here before –

Jarrod's thoughts were interrupted by a knocking at the door.

Everyone fell silent and turned to look at the door, eyes wide with terror. Jarrod was as afraid as everyone else. Everyone except Tasha, that is. Not only didn't she seemed concerned about the knocking, she actually smiled. She started walking toward the door, and without thinking, Jarrod grabbed hold of her arm to stop her.

"Sharks don't knock," she said. "Not even mutated ones."

Jarrod knew she was right, but he was still reluctant to let her go. He trusted her entirely – not that he could've articulated why, but he did. He released his grip on her arm and she continued to the door. Some of the other shouted for her to stop, others simply moaned in despair, but no one else tried to stop her. Susan aimed her reloaded shotgun at the door, and Pete gripped his freshly sharpened machete.

Tasha opened the door.

Jarrod flinched, expecting a horde of landsharks to come pouring into Susan's apartment, tearing Tasha to shreds as they came. But that didn't happen. The door swung open to reveal Boyd Campbell. The writer stood there, a dazed expression on his face, as if he was in shock but didn't realize it yet.

"Hi, everybody. Hell of a night, huh?"

* * * * *

Saul found Flotsam's back door, slammed it open, and burst out into the night. Once he was outside, he stopped. He'd gotten this far running on pure instinct for survival, but now that he'd successfully escaped the nightmares inside, his instincts seemed to shut down completely, leaving him at a loss.

No, he realized. His instincts were still operating just fine. They continued to scream that he needed to get the fuck away from there – *now!* The problem was they weren't any help right now. When he had been in the bar and those whatever-the-fuck-they were attacked, his instincts automatically knew he needed to get out, and right away, before those fucking monsters chewed through everyone else and got to him. But now he stood in an alley, and he could go left or right. There was nothing to indicate one direction was better – was *safer* – than another. And so his instincts had shrugged and turned the matter over to his conscious mind, as if to say, *We got you this far, buddy. Now it's up to you.*

"Thanks a fucking lot," he muttered.

Even with the back door closed behind him, he could still hear people screaming in the bar. People he'd abandoned, some of them friends and colleagues who right now were being torn apart by creatures that couldn't possibly exist.

They found those pliosaurs on that island, he reminded himself. *Who's to say what does or doesn't exist anymore?*

He knew he should feel guilty for running off like he had, but he didn't. He believed that humans had two opposite but effective strategies when it came to survival: working as a group for mutual benefit and looking out for number one. Which strategy you employed at which time depended entirely on the situation you found yourself in. He had no doubt which strategy was most effective in this case. He was alone and alive, and the others were inside, as a group, and dying. Quite horribly, too, from the sound of it. So yay for self-interest.

If his instincts weren't going to tell him what to do now, then he'd figure it out logically. He'd directed his first film at the tender age of twenty-six, and while he hadn't risen to the ranks of A-list directors – and likely never would – he'd worked steadily ever since, and there weren't many people in the industry who could say that. He was a survivor, and he intended to continue being one. He was also an artist, and as an artist, he knew the importance of making choices. Clear, *strong* choices. Even if a choice turned out to be a bad one, at least you'd made it, and that beat the hell out of indecisiveness. So that's what he would do now. Make a choice.

Right or left?

He'd read somewhere that when given a choice between right and left, most people chose right. Never one to go with the majority – case in point being how he hauled ass out of the bar and left everyone else to be shark chow – he chose left.

His nerves still jangled from the adrenaline in his system, but as he started jogging, his legs felt heavy as lead and his vision swam in and out of focus. His idea of a workout was walking on and off set, and he wasn't in the best of shape. It seemed his dash for survival had taken more out of him then he'd realized. He slowed to a walk and forced himself to breathe deeply and evenly. His vision sharpened, and while his legs still felt heavy, the sensation wasn't as bad as before. He almost laughed in relief. For a moment there he'd feared he'd overexerted himself and was experiencing the early symptoms of a heart attack. Wouldn't that have been a pisser? Escaping the Bar of Doom only to keel over in the alley because of a bum ticker?

As he reached the end of the alley, he stopped and cautiously poked his head out into the open. He wasn't about to set foot on the street if it was swarming with those fucking shark monsters. But the sidewalk was empty in both directions, and there was no sign of sharks in the street.

He grinned. *Looks like I made the right choice,* he thought as he stepped out of the alley. But as he did, he heard a soft *whssk-whssk-whssk* sound behind him. He turned and saw a shark coming toward him down the alley, the fish undulating like a caterpillar as it advanced, umbilical cord stretching behind it all the way to the other end of the alley. The creature was within twenty feet of him and closing fast. His old friend, adrenaline, decided to pay him another visit then, and his legs felt light once more and his body was filled with energy. No way was he going to end up in some mutant shark's belly tonight.

He started running, moving faster than he would've thought possible for a man of his age and fitness level. He made five steps before he felt a sledgehammer slam into his chest. At least, that's what it felt like. A bolt of fiery pain shot through his left arm, and his hand stiffened, fingers contorting as if he'd been afflicted with a sudden onset of arthritis. He knew the problem wasn't in his joints, though. It was his heart.

His legs gave out beneath him and he fell to the cobblestone street. He landed hard on his left side, and the impact caused the pain in his arm and chest to intensify. He cried out through gritted teeth, features contorted into a mask of agony.

Very funny, he thought to the universe. *Fucking hysterical, in fact.*

Darkness nibbled at the edges of his vision, and for a moment he thought he would be lucky enough to lose consciousness before the shark reached him. But his luck had run out.

He heard the shark scuttle out of the alley, felt it clamp its teeth into his right ankle. He thought the goddamned thing was going to eat him piece by piece, starting with his foot. But instead, its teeth pierced his flesh to the bone, and then it began pulling him backward. It dragged him back into the alley, all the way to Flotsam's rear door. They remained there for a moment – a director of cheap monster movies and an honest-to-Christ monster – waiting. A moment later, Saul knew why.

The back door exploded outward. A pair of sharks spilled into the alley, fell upon Saul, and began tearing hunks of meat off him. The shark that had brought him back joined in then, and Saul screamed and screamed until one of the sharks tore out his throat. Objectively, it didn't take very long for him to die, but it sure as shit felt like it did.

CHAPTER NINE

Inside the Mass, the part of the creature that thought of itself as Inez was pleased. The Hunters' upgraded design was working well, even better than she'd expected. And the attack on Flotsam was proceeding nicely. Several people had managed to survive the initial assault – which was, of course, exactly how she'd planned it. You can't kill off the entire cast before the end of the first act, not unless you wanted to completely lose your audience.

Shame about Saul, though. Still, it wasn't as if she needed a director anymore. She was doing just fine directing this particular production all by her lonesome.

Time for Act Two.

* * * * *

Pete said to Boyd what everyone was thinking.

"How the hell did you get up here in one piece?"

Tamara and Shari came back into the living room then. Tamara wore a Ramones T-shirt that was too-tight for her and a pair of black panties. Shari wore a white button shirt untucked over a pair of jeans shorts. Neither wore socks or shoes.

Boyd barely glanced at the two women before turning his attention to Pete.

"I'm the writer," he said. "They leave me alone because they want me to tell their story." His lips stretched into a mirthless smile that held more than a hint of madness. "Weird, huh?"

"Given the way the night's gone so far, I'd say that's par for the course," Tamara said.

Pete shot both Shari and Tamara a dark look. Shari looked away, but Tamara met his gaze and puckered her lips in a kissing motion.

If Boyd's the writer and the sharks are the monsters, I suppose that makes me the hero, Jarrod thought. *Might as well start acting like it. Right, Tasha?*

"Right," she said.

Jarrod grinned. "Gotcha!"

Tasha clapped a hand over her mouth and her eyes widened in alarm.

Don't worry. Your secret's safe with me. He turned away from Tasha and aloud he said, "Susan, is there a way to the roof?"

When Boyd had stepped into the room, she'd lowered the shotgun to her side, but she still held it tight.

"There's a fire escape outside. It doesn't go all the way to the roof, but there's an access ladder above it. It's a rickety-looking thing, but I think it'll hold."

"Why the hell do you want to go to the roof?" Pete asked.

"Our only other options are to stay here or go back downstairs and attempt to outrun the landsharks," Jarrod said. "If they could get into the bar, they can get in here. Hopefully, they won't be able to get at us on the roof."

"Hopefully?" Tamara said.

Jarrod shrugged. "Hopefully is the best we've got right now, I'm afraid."

"I am *not* going up a goddamned fire escape!" Bonnie sound close to full-fledged panic.

"Afraid of heights?" Tamara asked.

"You better fucking believe it!" Bonnie said.

Early in his career, Jarrod had made a western called *Ride Fast, Hang High.* The horses had supposedly been trained for filming. Not only were they patient with actors whose riding skills might be rudimentary at best, they didn't startle at sudden sounds – such as faux gunfire. Unfortunately, a couple of the horses were new to the wonderful world of playacting, and during a chase scene in which the hero rode hell for leather, trying to escape a gang of outlaws – one of whom was played by a young Jarrod – a couple of the horses panicked when the actors began firing their guns. Jarrod's horse was one of them. He'd had a bit more riding experience than his co-stars, and while it was a close thing, he'd managed to get his mount under control. What he remembered most about the incident was the absolutely insane terror in the animal's eyes, a primal wildness that had more in common with a raging wildfire than a living thing. He saw something similar in Bonnie's eyes now, and he knew that if she couldn't get her fear under control – at least a little – they'd never get her out of this room.

He reached out to Bonnie, intending to take both of her hands in his. She jerked her hands back as if she was afraid that he intended to attack her, but then she relaxed – just a little – and allowed him to enfold her hands within his own.

"We must leave, my dear, and I'm afraid we simply can't go without you. We need you to make us look good when the media interview us after this whole awful mess is over."

Bonnie looked at him for a moment without any indication that she'd understood a single word he'd said. But then she gave him a fragile smile and nodded. He returned the smile and gave her hands a squeeze.

Boyd spoke then.

"If we're going to leave, we should do it now. The sharks will be here soon." A pause. "They're smarter than you think."

Everyone looked at the man as if he was crazy – Jarrod included – but then Tasha said, "He's right," and Jarrod decided to take Boyd's warning seriously.

"Let's get moving," Pete said. He pointed his machete toward the living room window. "Is the fire escape out there?"

Susan nodded, and Pete stepped toward the window. He pulled the curtains aside, unlocked the window, and opened it. Pete wasn't really Jarrod's type, but he liked the man's take-charge attitude. But then, he supposed it was only to be expected from a stunt man, a literal man of action.

Pete stuck his head through the open window to take a look around. If this had been a movie, Jarrod would've expected Pete to let out a bloodcurdling scream as a mutated shark bit his head off. But that didn't happen, and Jarrod let out a breath that he hadn't realized he'd been holding.

Pete pulled his head back in and turned to look at them – excluding Shari and Tamara, whose eyes he hadn't met since they'd returned from Susan's bedroom.

"I'll go first. Susan, you want to bring up the rear?"

"Sure."

"Good. Everyone else will go between us. Take your time, make sure your footing is solid but keep moving. And I know it's a cliché, but don't look down."

"Are there any of *them* out there?" Bonnie asked.

"There's no sign of them," Pete said.

Tasha stood on her tiptoes to whisper in Jarrod's ear.

"It wants us to go to the roof, and it's afraid if we see sharks on the ground, we won't leave the apartment."

Jarrod wondered what *it* was, but there was no time to worry about that now. He'd ask Tasha later – if they were both still alive then.

Pete climbed through the window onto the fire escape. Without turning to see if anyone followed, he started heading upward. Tamara moved to go next, but Shari cut her off with a glare and followed after her husband. Tamara seemed amused by Shari's actions rather than upset, and she went next.

"I'll go second to last," Boyd said. "I'll be in a better position to observe that way."

Jarrod and Susan exchanged a look, and the woman shrugged as if to say *Whatever the crazy fucker wants.*

Jarrod had continued to hold onto Bonnie's hands, and now he let go of them. Only for a moment, though. He took her right hand and without being prompted, Tasha took her left.

"Come along, dear," Jarrod said. "Tasha and I will help you."

The wild fear was back in her eyes, but she allowed Tasha and Jarrod to lead her toward the window. Tasha went first, and she gently pulled Bonnie after her. The makeup artist hesitated a moment, but she went through. Jarrod – relieved they'd gotten Bonnie this far – climbed out onto the fire escape with them. The metal was covered with rust, but the structure seemed sturdy enough. He looked upward and saw Pete, Shari, and Tamara were already near the rooftop. The fire escape rattled as they ascended, filling the night air with noise. The racket worried Jarrod. Weren't sharks supposed to be drawn by noise? No, it was vibrations in the water that attracted them. He didn't know if the animals even had ears. However they sensed vibrations, could they do so through the air? He didn't think so, but then, these were hardly normal sharks, were they? Who knew what kind of senses they had or what they were capable of physically?

Tasha began climbing the fire escape's stairs and Bonnie followed. Jarrod could see Bonnie was shaking like a leaf in a hurricane-force gale, but she kept moving, which he took as a good sign. He followed, making sure to grip the thin metal railing tightly. He felt feverish and lightheaded – no doubt his body's response to the stress of the situation – and he wanted to avoid passing out, falling off the fire escape, and plummeting down to the alley below. Hardly a dignified death. Besides, if he was the hero of this adventure, it was his duty to survive – at least until the story's climax.

Boyd and Susan followed after Jarrod, and now all eight of them were on the fire escape. Jarrod could feel the metal vibrate beneath his hands and his feet, and he hoped the old fire escape could withstand having so many people climb it at once. He imagined the bolts that held the metal construction in the building beginning to pull away from ancient, crumbling brick, pictured the entire thing falling away from the building and pitching them all off, imagined them tumbling toward the ground where the sharks – who'd arrived soon after they'd begun climbing – waited for their heaven-sent feast. But the fire escape held, although it did feel more than a little wobbly by the time Jarrod reached the access ladder to the roof. Pete, Shari, Tamara, and Tasha had already climbed up it and were standing on the roof, save from the sharks. At least for the moment. But Bonnie had stopped halfway up the access ladder and refused to go any farther.

"I can't do it!" she said, a sobbing hitch in her voice. "I *can't!*"

The woman had successfully fought her acrophobia up to this point. But now that she was out in the air and exposed, her fear had taken hold of her once more.

"Of course you can," Jarrod said. It took every ounce of acting skill and experience at his command to make his voice sound calm and reassuring, when all he really wanted to do was shout for Bonnie to quit fucking around and hurry the hell up before the goddamned sharks figured out how to climb the fire escape.

"You've done makeup for how many actors in your career?" he asked. "Hundreds, I'd wager."

At first he thought she wasn't going to respond, but she said, "Yeah. Something like that."

"And out of all these people, how many were thundering assholes or insufferable cunts who made your job harder than it had to be?"

She surprised him by letting out a strangled laugh.

"Most of them," she said.

"If you can deal with all of them, then you can certainly climb a few more rungs to get to the roof. The others are waiting there to help you. All you need to do is start climbing again."

She didn't move for several seconds, and Jarrod began to think he would end up yelling at her after all, but then slowly, hesitantly, she began to climb once more.

The people on the roof shouted encouragement to her, as did Jarrod and Susan. Boyd just watched her, silent and expressionless.

Jarrod didn't know what happened. Maybe the ladder – a narrow, rusted thing that didn't look strong enough to hold a child let alone a full-grown adult – pulled away from the wall several inches, startling Bonnie. Or maybe she was sweating so much in her terror that her hands slipped off the rungs. Or maybe she was shaking so badly that she couldn't make her hands grip the next rung tightly enough. Or – and this was the worst possibility of all – maybe the idea of falling and dying quickly sounded like a better option to her than being torn apart by monster sharks. Whichever the case, Bonnie fell off the ladder.

Jarrod tried to catch her, but her left shoulder hit the edge of the fire escape's railing, and she bounced out of reach. He watched, horrified as she plummeted to the ground, and he didn't understand why she was so quiet as she fell. Maybe she was too scared to scream. Or maybe her falling had taken her by surprise and she hadn't had time to process what was happening to her.

As Jarrod looked down, he saw that a pair of sharks had taken up position below the fire escape, their umbilical cords stretching toward opposite ends of the alley, indicating the direction they'd each come from. The sharks looked up at Bonnie as she fell, and Jarrod was put in mind of the way a dog watches a treat its owner is about to toss to it. These creatures had the same laser-sharp focus and air of eager, barely restrained anticipation.

Before Bonnie could hit the ground, the sharks leaped upward to catch hold of her in midair. Jarrod had no idea how the damn things could jump with those tiny insect-like legs of theirs, but they managed. One shark caught hold of Bonnie's right leg, the other her left arm. They bit down, getting a good hold on her limbs, when they landed with a combined thud, the sharks yanked and tore Bonnie's limbs from their sockets in sprays of blood.

Bonnie screamed then – loud and high – but her screams didn't last long. When the sharks finished with Bonnie, they looked upward at Jarrod and the others, and while the creatures were incapable of anything even approximating human expression, Jarrod couldn't escape the impression the fucking beasts were grinning.

* * * * *

Jarrod wanted to turn away so he wouldn't have to watch the landsharks devour Bonnie's remains, but he also felt compelled to stand witness for the woman. Looking away would seem like a betrayal of her memory somehow. Tasha's hand slipped around his and squeezed.

I'll watch with you, she said in his mind, and while he would've preferred to spare her the sight of the sharks eating their friend, he was grateful for Tasha's presence. The others leaned over the edge and also watched, perhaps feeling the same sense of responsibility that Jarrod did, or perhaps out of an instinct to know one's enemy.

The sharks each gobbled several organs that had spilled from the two halves of Bonnie's body, but that was all. They then got a grip on the halves with their teeth and began dragging the halves backward, tugging them toward the two different ends of the alley. When they reached the separate streets, they continued on until lost from sight. When the creatures were gone, all that remained were twin trails of blood covering the floor of the alley from one side to the other.

"Where the hell are the damn things going?" Pete asked.

"They're taking the meat back home," Tasha said. "To feed the Mass." She looked around suddenly. "Wait. Did I say that out loud?" She glanced at Jarrod. "I'm starting to lose track of which voice I'm using."

She showed no sign of letting go of Jarrod's hand any time soon, and that was fine with him. Right now, he could use all the support he could get. The weariness that was a symptom of his leukemia hit him full force then, the aftermath of the adrenaline and physical exertion of escaping Flotsam and Susan's apartment. He felt suddenly dizzy, and he said, "I need to sit down." He let go of Tasha's hand then basically fell onto the roof ass-first. The impact jarred his spine and made his teeth clack together, but he barely noticed, and anyway, he was too fucking tired to care.

"Are you all right?" Tamara said. "You're not stroking out on us or anything, are you?" Jarrod thought dying from a sudden massive stroke would be preferable to dying slowly while cancer ate him from the inside out. But given the way the evening was going, he doubted he'd live long enough for either to happen. He'd most likely end up in a landshark's belly before the night was over. That, or be fed to this Mass Tasha had spoken of. He didn't know which would be worse – being eaten alive by his own renegade body or by mutant sharks. The sharks, he supposed, but that didn't mean he wanted to find out.

Boyd stared out toward the ocean with an expression of contemplative awe, but everyone else focused their attention on Jarrod, worry writ plainly on their faces. Except Pete, who was looking at Tasha, the newly sharpened machete gripped tightly in his hand. His expression was one of angry suspicion, and Jarrod feared the man might attack her.

"How do you know what those sharks are doing, and what the fuck is the Mass?" Pete demanded. He took a step toward Tasha, not a very big one, perhaps even a subconscious one, and he raised the machete until it was level with his waist. Still not in attack position, Jarrod thought, but ready to go there if necessary. Everyone turned to look at Tasha then, their expressions mirroring Pete's suspicion.

Tasha looked from one to the other in turn. She opened her mouth to speak, but nothing came out. How could it? Jarrod thought she had a lifetime of practice keeping her psychic abilities secret.

Jarrod rose unsteadily to his feet, but once on them, he remained standing, and he considered that a victory.

"It seems our dear Ms. Bates is a telepath. She can sense what those creatures are thinking."

"Is that true?" Susan asked Tasha.

Tasha nodded. Then she pointed at them one at a time and spoke.

"Susan – you're wondering if your girlfriend on the other side of town is okay, but you're too afraid to call in case she doesn't answer."

"Boyd – the Mass has chosen you to document its activities, and you're already thinking of ways to turn tonight's madness into a million-dollar script. Maybe even one you'll get to direct."

Boyd didn't look at Tasha as she said this, just kept looking toward the ocean. But he acknowledged her words with a nod.

Jarrod looked at Boyd and raised an eyebrow. "Really, Boyd? A screenwriter who has a secret desire to direct? Could you get any more cliché?"

Boyd turned toward Jarrod, gave him a half smile and shrugged, as if to say, *So I'm cliché. Big fucking deal.*

Tasha continued.

"Tamara – you're hoping Shari and Pete will be able to get past your affairs with each of them. You genuinely like them both and wish them no harm."

"Shari – you're picturing yourself kicking Pete in the chest and sending him tumbling over the building's edge to a horde of hungry sharks below."

"Pete – you're thinking I'm kind of a spooky chick and you're wondering if I'll fuck you if we survive this night."

Pete's face reddened with embarrassment, and Shari said, "For Christ's sake, Pete, can't you stop thinking about your goddamned cock long enough to –"

She broke off, eyes widening. She pointed to the opposite side of the roof and screamed.

Everyone, even Boyd, looked where Shari was pointing and saw a pair of landsharks climbing over the building's edge and onto the roof with their tiny insect feet, umbilical cords trailing behind them.

While Jarrod and the others had been busy watching Bonnie die, another pair of sharks had gained the roof via the fire escape on the building's other side, and they were now trundling toward the small group of tasty humans, jaws snapping, crimson eyes gleaming.

Susan raised her shotgun to her shoulder, aimed at one of the sharks, and squeezed the trigger. The creature's head exploded in a cloud of red mist, and meat chunks sprayed the air. The landshark hit the roof, dead.

"Got you!" Susan shouted, as much in relief as triumph.

Not to be outdone, Pete stepped toward the second shark, machete held high. As a stunt man, Pete was perfectly suited for battling a mutant creature. He was fit and used to taking stupid risks.

"Cut its cord!" Tasha shouted.

Jarrod didn't see how Pete could get at the cord before the shark could sink its teeth into him. The man needed a distraction, and Jarrod decided to give him one. Jarrod began walking toward the second shark, unsteadily at first but with increasing confidence. It seemed his old body wasn't quite ready to give out on him yet. He moved at an angle designed to draw the shark away from Pete. Jarrod still felt too weak to run, but that didn't mean he was helpless. He was an actor, and he'd performed under worse conditions than these. Well, perhaps that was an exaggeration, but not by much. He decided to go with a speech written for one of his favorite characters, vampire hunter Robert Fischer, from *Night of the Blood Thieves*. He spoke in a booming voice, hoping to attract the shark's attention.

"You unholy creatures may believe yourselves superior to us mere mortals, and in many respects you'd be right. You're stronger, faster, and more ruthless than we are. But we have one quality which you will never be able to match us, a simple four-letter word: L-O-V-E!"

These were the corniest lines he'd ever delivered in a film, which was saying something given the sort of movies he made – and it had originally required seventeen takes to get the lines right because he kept bursting into giggles before he could get to the end of the speech.

Corny or not, the lines had their intended effect. The landshark veered toward Jarrod and increased its speed, as if personally offended by the horrible dialogue he'd spoken.

Everyone's a critic, Jarrod thought.

CHAPTER TEN

Grady Silva had been head of Bridgewater's sheriff department for the last twelve years. Before that he'd worked as a cop in Houston, and while he sometimes missed living in the city, overall small-town life suited him. Bridgewater had taken a real hit from Hurricane Janae, and it looked like the town would never recover, which was sad, but Grady figured towns had lifespans the same as people, and while Bridgewater might not be dead, it sure as shit was on life support. But he had less than two years until he could retire, and he figured if Bridgewater could keep limping along until then, he and his wife could return to Houston after he retired. Or maybe they'd settle in another small town, one that had a little more life left in it than Bridgewater.

The movie people had brought some welcome excitement to town, and Grady and his deputies had enjoyed watching them work while providing "security" that the production really didn't need. That was the reason he was out tonight "working late." The movie people liked to hang out at Flotsam's when the day's shooting was done, and he liked to stop by and shoot the shit with them for an hour or two. He wasn't starstruck by any means, and while he'd seen several of Jarrod Drayton's movies over the years, he wasn't a fan of horror. He liked talking with the movie people because they were a change of pace from his job, which after Janae had become mostly keeping people out of empty and condemned buildings, usually kids who wanted places to drink, smoke pot, and screw.

He wore his uniform when stopping at Flotsam's so he'd look as if he were taking a break in his shift instead of making a special trip. His wife made fun of him for trying to play it cool. *You're not fooling anyone, Grady. You know that, right?* But he didn't care. Besides, he thought he looked good in his uniform, even if he could stand to lose some weight. He'd caught Tamara Young checking him out a couple of times, and while he knew he was probably a fool to imagine she'd be interested in an old guy like him, he entertained fantasies of banging her before the film shoot wrapped. But who knows? Stranger things had happened, right?

He drove his cruiser down Goodwin Street, heading toward Sailor's Walk. As he drew closer to the bar, he thought it odd that he didn't encounter any other traffic, either vehicular or pedestrian. Yeah, it was a weeknight, and even on weekends Sailor's Walks wasn't as busy as it had been before Janae, but usually there were more people around than this. It was weird, and while Grady was no one's idea of a deductive genius, he'd been a cop long enough to know when something wasn't right.

When he reached the intersection of Goodwin and Hines Street, he turned right. He was officially in Sailor's Walk now, and the cruiser juddered as its tires rolled over cobblestones. Grady hated these fucking things, but somebody on the town council must've figured cobblestone streets were quaint and would attract tourists. A dumbass idea if he'd ever heard one, and a literal pain in the ass, too.

When he was within a block of Flotsam, his headlights illuminated something strange – three fleshy-looking hoses that emerged from an alley onto Hines Street and stretched off in the bar's direction.

What the fuck?

Grady slowed and stopped ten feet from the nearest hose. He parked and got out, leaving the cruiser's engine running and the lights on. He wore his gun – never without it when in uniform – and he automatically unsnapped the thin leather strap that kept the weapon secured in its side holster. When you were a law officer, you didn't necessarily expect trouble whenever you stopped to check something out, but you were an idiot if you didn't allow for the possibility.

He swept his gaze around the area but saw no one in the immediate vicinity. When he reached the first hose, he knelt to get a closer look at it. Whatever these things were, they smelled like shit, their odor a combination of seawater and rotting meat. Their rubbery substance was slick with some kind of mucus and were shot through with thread dark veins. He knew then that they weren't hoses, weren't something that had been manufactured. They had been *grown*. They were alive – or rather part of something alive.

He drew his 9 millimeter and touched the muzzle to the hose . . . no, the *cord* closest to him. He pressed a little, and the cord gave beneath the barrel, but it returned to its previous shape the instant he pulled the gun away. A ropey line of mucus stretched from the cord to the gun barrel, and Grady gave the weapon a disgusted shake to flick the snot-like crap off his gun.

The cords began quivering then, and Grady quickly straightened and took a couple of steps back. The cords' motion became more pronounced, and Grady found himself thinking that he should get back in the cruiser, close the door, and get the hell out of there. He had no rational reason for feeling this way. Just more cop intuition. But he didn't listen to it, told himself that whatever these damn things were, they weren't dangerous. Besides, it was his job to figure out what the hell they were and what – if anything – needed to be done about them.

A moment later he heard a sort of whispery-rustling sound that reminded him of broom bristles sliding across a hard surface. The sound grew louder, and as he turned to look in its direction, he saw a trio of shapes – larger and low to the ground – approaching.

Sharks, he thought. *Motherfucking sharks.*

But as bizarre as it was to see three sharks trundling along on land like miniature streamlined tanks, equally as strange – and far more disturbing – was what the sharks carried in their mouths: bloody pieces of a human body. One carried an arm, one a leg, and the other a torso. They all had organs and viscera clamped between their jaws as well.

At first he was unable to comprehend what he was seeing. It was too unreal, too nightmarish. But then he realized what was happening and let out a laugh. The film crew were doing a night shoot! He'd thought the pliosaur was the only monster in the movie, but evidently these shark things were in it, too. Those weird hoses connected to the creatures' backs were probably power cords or hydraulics or something. He imagined they'd use CGI to erase the cords from the final footage. The sharks were pretty damn slick effects, a hell of a lot more realistic-looking than that dinosaur.

These things were scary enough to carry a movie all by themselves. He'd mention it to Inez when he saw her at the bar. Who knows? If she took his suggestion, she might give him a screen credit as a consultant. How awesome would that be?

Grady glanced around, looking for the film crew, but he saw no one. He told himself they were just well hidden, staying out of the way as the scene was filmed, but he knew that was bullshit. He'd hung around enough during the filming of *Devourer from the Deep* to know the crew was *always* around, even on modest production like this one. Besides, even with the street lights on, it was too dark to film here. *Maybe they're not shooting,* he thought. *Maybe this is some kind of special effects rehearsal.* But if so, there would still be *some* crew around. At the very least, Enrique would be here to monitor the sharks' performance. But there was no one on the street besides him.

The sharks continued gliding toward him, and as they did, he got a better look at the body parts they carried. One in particular, a woman's head, caught his attention. It looked like Bonnie, the production's makeup person. Maybe it had been some kind of gag to make the fake head resemble hers. Or maybe she was going to have a bit part as a victim of these monsters. But the head looked real, and when the sharks drew even with him, the head – which Grady could see was attached to the body only by a thin strip of meat – came free and bounced on the cobblestones toward him. It came to a stop at his feet, and he knew then that he was looking at the real thing. Since coming to Bridgewater, Grady had never fired his weapon in the line of duty. But he didn't hesitate. He raised his gun, trained the barrel on the shark carrying Bonnie's now headless torso, and fired three quick rounds into the thing. The impact of the bullets knocked the shark off course, and it tried to correct, weaving as it struggled to continue on before finally stopping and rolling onto its side. Bonnie's torso slipped from its jaws and fell to the cobblestones with a wet *smack*.

The other shark didn't turn back, didn't so much as slow. It continued on into the night, carrying Bonnie's legs and trunk to whatever its final destination was. Grady forgot about the thing and focused his entire attention on the shark he'd brought down. He kept his weapon trained on the damn thing as he carefully stepped past

Bonnie's head. An image flashed through his mind then, of him accidentally kicking Bonnie's head in an attempt to go by, the head bouncing away across the cobblestones like a grisly soccer ball. But he made it past Bonnie's head without incident and stepped close to the dead shark. At least he *hoped* it was dead. Those weird pink gill fronds were still, and the creature didn't appear to be breathing. But he'd never killed a shark before, let alone one like *this*, and he wasn't certain how to tell if the shark still clung to life or not. All he could think of was to give the thing a hard kick and see if it reacted. He did so, but other than quivering once from the force of the blow, the shark remained motionless. The thing gave off a foul odor, part saltwater, part rotting fish, part something Grady couldn't identify. Its hide was strange, shot through with crimson threads that looked like capillaries, its eyes were red, and of course there were the gill fronds, the weird little growths on its belly like tiny insect legs, and the long cord embedded behind its dorsal fin. The cord was so long that Grady couldn't see the other end of it. It stretched off into the distance, woven around corners of buildings and between streetlights.

He didn't know what the fuck this goddamned thing was, but he did know one thing. Whatever was going on here was above his pay grade. This was a job for the state police. Hell, maybe for the FBI or Homeland Security. He lowered his gun and with his free hand reached for his phone. He had the device halfway to his ear when the dead shark's cord began to tremble. It tore free from the shark's body in a spray of blood, then raised up like a cobra, head swaying back and forth. But instead of a head, it had a wickedly barbed hook on the tip. Grady didn't think much of his chances to shoot the barb. It was a relatively small target, and it was in constant motion, but he had to try. He managed to raise his gun once more, but the cord moved faster. It undulated in a sharp motion, like a whip, and the barb shot toward Grady, moving too swiftly for him to react. The barb arced behind him, found the base of his spine, and penetrated flesh and bone with surgical precision. The pain was unbelievable, and accompanying it was a white light which obliterated his vision. His body stiffened and remained that way until the light receded and his vision cleared. At that moment, the consciousness that called itself Grady Silva ceased to exist, and his body became an empty vessel, awaiting the Mass' command.

A loud noise came from the northwest, a sound that Grady would've recognized as a shotgun blast. The consciousness that now controlled him knew exactly what had made that sound, and she wanted Grady to investigate. Still holding onto his weapon, the sheriff's body began shuffling away, heading toward Flotsam.

* * * * *

Jarrod felt an almost irresistible urge to turn and run. It seemed even a dying body wanted to protect whatever life remained to it. But he forced himself to stay where he was, and he kept his gaze fixed on the oncoming creature. If a real-life monster was going to kill the King of Schlock Horror, Jarrod intended to meet his death without flinching.

As the shark moved past Pete, the stuntman stepped forward and swung the machete at the creature's umbilicus, close to where it emerged from the shark's body. Metal bit into meat with a *thunk* and clear liquid sprayed from the wound. The creature surprised Jarrod by releasing what sounded like an entirely too-human scream. A *woman's* scream. The shark whirled around to go after its attacker, but Pete wasn't going to give it a chance. Before the creature could turn on him, he yanked the machete free – causing even more clear liquid to gush from the wound – and struck the umbilicus a second time. The machete severed the cord this time, and fluid spurted from both ends. The pressure of the flow rapidly diminished, and the shark slowed. It continued toward Pete, jaws snapping halfheartedly now, as if it was only trying to bite him out of reflex. Then, when the creature was less than a foot from Pete, it collapsed and lay motionless. The strange pink fronds growing from its gills immediately began to blacken and shrivel, and the clear fluid leaking from the remnants of the umbilicus attached to its body became mixed with blood.

Jarrod and the others walked over to Pete, Boyd included. Susan kept her shotgun trained on the shark's head in case it had some life in it yet, but it didn't so much as twitch. Tamara and Shari – who were now the ones holding hands, Jarrod noted – remained several feet back, but Jarrod, Tasha, Boyd, and Susan joined Pete next to the landshark's corpse. Now that Jarrod was close to Pete, he could see that the man was soaked with the fluid that had gushed from the dying shark's wounds.

"What the hell *is* that shit on you?" Shari said. She seemed to realize she was holding Tamara's hand then, and she quickly let go. Jarrod was certain Pete saw, but the man chose not to remark on it.

"Believe it or not, I think it's seawater," Pete said.

Jarrod leaned closer to the man and inhaled. Sure enough, he smelled saltwater.

"It makes sense," Boyd said. "It's the reverse of a human diving underwater. We take oxygen with us to breathe. These creatures bring seawater with them. It probably helps them stay hydrated, too."

Boyd began walking slowly around the dead shark, examining it closely. *He's taking mental notes,* Jarrod thought, *for when he writes about tonight.* Jarrod wasn't bothered overmuch by the man's actions, but rather by the total lack of emotion on his face. People had died tonight, a *lot* of people, among them some of their colleagues. Tony and Nina. Saul, presumably. And poor Bonnie. Inez hadn't shown up at Flotsam tonight. Who knew if she was still alive? But Boyd appeared entirely unfazed by what had taken place this night, nor did he seem repulsed by the bizarre creatures which had attacked them.

Tasha had said the Mass – whatever that was exactly – had chosen Boyd to make a record of tonight's events. Had this Mass done something to Boyd which had affected his mind? Was he in shock? Or had Boyd been like this the entire time, an unfeeling void of a human, and they were only now seeing the true person behind the façade?

"A bit of all three," Tasha said.

Jarrod nodded, accepting this.

"Look!" Shari shouted.

Everyone – except Boyd, who continued his examination of the dead shark – looked to Shari. She was pointing at the detached umbilicus. Up to this point it had lain limply on the roof, but now it quivered and slowly retracted, picking up speed as it moved backward, until it slipped over the edge and was gone.

Jarrod turned to Tasha.

"Is it going back to the Mass?" he asked.

"Yes. All the sharks are attached to it by those cords."

Pete scowled at her.

"You really expect us to believe you're some kind of psychic?" he said.

"I don't have to *expect* anything. I know you all believe. Besides, is my being psychic any more fucked up than a bunch of homicidal landsharks?"

"No," Susan said. "It's actually pretty normal compared to that."

Tamara and Shari nodded. Pete looked unhappy, but he didn't disagree.

"Do you know what's happening?" Tamara asked Tasha. "If you help get us out of this alive, I promise to give you the best orgasm you've ever had."

Both Shari and Pete gave Tamara dirty looks, but she didn't appear to notice. Boyd finished his inspection of the dead shark and walked over to join the others.

Tasha looked extremely uncomfortable, and Jarrod thought he understood why. Not only wasn't she used to people knowing her secret, she wasn't used to people looking at her differently *because* they knew. When he'd first started acting nearly forty years ago, gay people were reluctant, and often too frightened, to be open about their sexuality. Even in the entertainment industry, which was far more accepting of different lifestyles than the culture as a whole, actors kept their real selves hidden so it wouldn't end up costing them work. Jarrod had been one of those people, afraid to let the world know who he really was, worried audiences wouldn't accept him as a redoubtable hero if they knew he was gay, and equally worried they'd equate being gay with being evil when he played villains. Eventually, he'd gotten to a point where he was comfortable being who and what he truly was in public, but it hadn't been easy. His situation and Tasha's might not be analogous, but he thought he had an inkling of how she felt.

Tasha gave him a grateful smile. "You do." Then she turned to Tamara. "I sensed the Mass earlier today, although I only knew it was a presence somewhere out in the ocean. Once the sharks attacked Flotsam, I was able to pick up a little more because they were so close. I got the main creature's name, or at least a concept that comes close to how it views itself."

"The Mass," Susan said, and Tasha nodded.

"And I know the sharks are connected to it. They're part of it, kind of like . . . like our hands. We can reach out with them, grab food, and bring it to our mouths to feed ourselves. We can also use our hands to protect our bodies. That what the sharks – the *Hunters* – do for the Mass."

"Why is it attacking Bridgewater?" Shari asked. "There's plenty of food in the sea, isn't there? Why even bother coming on land?"

"I don't know," Tasha said. "It's hard to touch the Mass' mind. It doesn't have a brain like ours, doesn't think like us. It's old, like *prehistoric* old. Its type of intelligence predates ours by millions of years. But something about it's changed recently. I can't figure out what. Sometimes it almost feels like its mind is familiar to me, but other times it's utterly alien. I don't understand."

Jarrod could feel the frustration coming off Tasha. Not only could he see it in her expression and hear it in her voice, but he could feel it in his mind as well. The girl could transmit as well as receive.

Up to this point, the umbilicus of the shark Susan had shot had remained motionless. But now it sprang to life and tore free of its host's body, revealing a nasty-looking barb on its tip.

"Be careful!" Tasha warned. "It wants a new host, and since we're the only ones around –"

"It's not exactly spoiled for choice," Jarrod finished.

As if Jarrod's voice attracted it, the barb flew toward him, snaked around his back, and penetrated his spine.

The least you could've done is bought me dinner first, he thought. The pain was bad, but he'd been living with pain as his constant companion for months now, and he could take it.

Tasha was the closest to Jarrod, and she grabbed hold of the cord with both hands and yanked, attempting to pull the barb out of Jarrod. This hurt worse and he couldn't stop himself from letting out a cry of pain. The cord went slack for a moment then, and Jarrod wondered if Tasha had used some kind of psychic whammy on it. But then it withdrew from his body, the exit hurting a hell of a lot more than its entrance had. The cord writhed in Tasha's grip and Jarrod feared that if it got free, it would attempt to pierce her spine. He stepped forward, raised his right foot, and brought it down on the cord at a point less than five feet from the barb.

"Pete!" he called.

The stunt man didn't need further explanation. He dashed forward, raised his machete, and chopped at a section of the cord between Jarrod and Tasha. The cord was tight against the roof, and Pete was able to cut through it with a single strike. Seawater mixed with blood gushed from both ends of the severed cord, and the part in Tasha's hand kept whipping around for several seconds before its movements slowed and it finally fell limp.

Tasha threw the section of umbilicus to the roof with an expression of disgust.

"The damn thing feels like it's covered in snot," she said. She knelt and wiped her hands on the roof as best she could.

"The Mass can control *people*, too?" Shari said. "Jesus Christ."

A voice came shouting up from the alley then.

"Hey, anyone up there need help?"

CHAPTER ELEVEN

Jarrod recognized that voice, and he wasn't the only one.

"It's Grady!" Tamara said.

"Did you fuck him, too?" Pete muttered, but Tamara acted like she didn't hear him. She rushed to the building's edge, moving so fast Jarrod feared she might pitch over the side. She didn't, though. She put her hands palm down on the ledge and peered down into the alley.

"Grady! Hey, it's us!"

She raised a hand and waved it vigorously in the air, as if afraid the sheriff might miss seeing her otherwise. The others hurried over to join her, except Tasha, who hung back, frowning, and Jarrod, who remained at her side.

"Is something wrong?" Jarrod asked.

"I don't know. Maybe?" She gave him a rueful smiled. "Psychic powers aren't known for their precision."

"Seems to me you've been doing fine so far. Let's see what's happening." Jarrod put a hand on Tasha's shoulder and the two of them went over to join the others.

Sure enough, the man standing in the alley looking up at them was Grady Silva, and he was armed with a pistol. If the man hadn't been armed, Jarrod figured he would've been shark food by now. There was something odd about the way he was standing, though. Jarrod couldn't put his finger on it at first, but then he realized what it was. Grady stood next to the opposite building, so close that his back was practically pressed up against it. It was almost as if he was trying to protect his back –

– or hide it.

"How did you all end up on the roof?" Grady called.

"Landshark attack!" Susan shouted down.

"Lot of that going around," Grady said. "My people have got the area pretty well cleared out, so it's safe to come down." He paused, then added, "Unless you want to stay up there until morning, just to be on the safe side."

"No way *I'm* staying," Shari said. "Those fuckers can climb!" Without looking at either Pete or Tamara, she went to the fire escape and started heading down.

The others looked at Jarrod.

"It might be our best bet," he said. "Once we're on the ground, we can head inland. The sharks' umbilical cords can only stretch so far, right?"

He didn't need to convince them any further. One by one, they followed Shari down the fire escape, leaving Jarrod and Tasha behind.

Jarrod looked at Tasha. "If you want to stay up here, I'll remain with you," he said.

For an instant, he thought she was going to take him up on his offer, but then she gave her head a shake, as if to dismiss her doubts, and she stepped onto the fire escape. A moment later, Jarrod followed.

The fire escape seemed even less sturdy than it had on their way up, but it held and several minutes later everyone was standing in the alley with Grady.

Once on the ground, Tasha moved close to Jarrod and stood half behind him.

"This isn't right," she whispered. "This isn't *right*."

Grady's gaze fixed on Tasha, and his mouth stretched into a slow smile. He raised his gun and pointed it at them.

"What was your first clue?" he said.

Jarrod stared at Grady, his mouth literally hanging open. This time when the man spoke, the voice wasn't his. It was Inez's. And that's when Jarrod saw the umbilicus on the ground, pressed close to the wall where it would be harder to see from the roof. One end of the cord stretched to the alley's mouth and out into the street, while the other disappeared behind Grady's feet, no doubt continuing up his legs to the back of his spine. Grady belonged to the Mass now. But why the hell was he speaking in *Inez's* voice?

"Put your weapons on the ground and slide them over to me," Grady said.

Susan and Pete glanced at each other. Both held their weapons at their sides – they'd thought Grady was a friend – and Jarrod guessed they were checking each other's willingness to risk getting shot before attempting a move against Grady. Neither must have thought much of their chances, for they did as Grady ordered. When the shotgun and rusty machete rested at his feet, Grady stepped over them, blocking them with his body.

Smart move, Jarrod thought. Anyone who made an attempt to get the weapons back would have to go through Grady and end up getting shot.

"I know you all have a lot of questions, but I *loathe* gratuitous exposition sequences. Suffice it to say that I am now the Mass, and the Mass is me. And tonight we're making the greatest real-life horror movie in history."

Not only was the voice Inez's, but Grady spoke with her speech inflections and cadences. And his body language mirrored Inez's as well.

Jarrod glanced at Tasha, but she didn't take her eyes off Grady. But Grady – or Inez – was looking at him.

"And what horror movie would be complete without the great Jarrod Drayton? You play the hero in this one, Jarrod. A tragic hero, as it turns out. Imagine my surprise when I tried to join with you and discovered your body isn't exactly your best friend right now."

The others turned to look at Jarrod.

"What's he – she – talking about?" Tamara asked.

"I have leukemia," Jarrod said. Speaking the words was easier than he'd thought it would be, and more than that, it was freeing.

"Oh my god," Susan said. "I'm so sorry."

"It's okay, love. I've made my peace with it. And we have bigger fish to fry right now."

"A fish joke," Inez said appreciatively. "Nice."

Pete's gaze wasn't focused on Jarrod but rather on Grady's face. Jarrod saw Pete tensing his body and he knew the man was considering making a grab for the sheriff's weapon. Jarrod couldn't fault Pete's bravery, but he thought going for the gun would be a mistake. Whatever the Mass – or Inez – had done to Grady, the man continued to move normally. There was no reason to think his reflexes were hindered in any way, which meant that if Pete went for the weapon, there was an excellent chance he'd end up catching a bullet in his gut.

"By the way, what do you think of the sharks?" Inez said. "I had to do a bit of genetic engineering to make them landworthy. It wasn't easy – took quite a lot out of me, in fact – but I think it was worth it."

Pete moved forward, just an inch, but both Shari and Tamara put hands on his shoulders to stop him. This little domestic drama would've been fascinating to watch, Jarrod thought, if it wasn't for all the goddamned monsters.

Tasha had been silent for several minutes. At first, Jarrod thought it was because she was scared, but when he turned to look at her, he saw an expression of fierce concentration on her face. Her gaze was focused intently on Grady, and Jarrod understood she was attempting to read his mind. Or Inez's. He wished he could somehow help her. The more they learned about the Mass – what it was and what it wanted – the better their chances of surviving the night would be.

"Things have been going great so far," Grady said with Inez's voice. "Lots of screaming, lots of dying, blood spilled all over the place – not to mention an absolute *fuck-ton* of tasty-tasty meat. But it's time to increase the stakes, make them more personal, you know what I'm saying? So here's the deal."

Jarrod sensed movement out of the corner of his eye, and he turned to see a pair of landsharks enter from one end of the alley. He turned to look in the opposite direction and saw another pair of sharks approaching from that direction.

Inez continued. "You're going to select one of you to get torn to pieces by my four friends here. If you don't select someone, you're *all* going to die. And here's the kicker: the vote has to be *unanimous*."

The sharks stopped five feet away from Jarrod and the others, blocking off their only routes of escape. Grady's mouth widened into a mirthless grin, displaying his teeth.

"Isn't this just fucking *brilliant*? I'll give you five minutes to decide, and your time starts –"

Grady/Inez broke off, frowning. He cocked his head to the side, as if he was listening for something. He remained like that for several seconds, then his head snapped upright and his gaze focused on Tasha with laser-like intensity.

"Well now, aren't *you* a surprise? Who would've guessed an unassuming little nobody like you would turn out to be a goddamned psychic? Talk about a plot twist! You're good, Tasha. *Very* good. I almost didn't feel you sneaking around in my mind, trying to discover my secrets, hoping to learn if I have any weaknesses you can exploit," She lowered her voice to a whisper. "Guess what? I don't *have* any. I wouldn't have survived since the proverbial dawn of time if I had."

Grady's brow furrowed in thought.

"Well, this certainly changes things. My little game seems like pretty small potatoes compared to discovering that one of my film crew is an honest-to-Christ psychic. That's okay, though. No, it's better than okay. It's fan-fucking-*tastic!* When you're a producer, you need to be flexible. Adaptable. You need to know how to improvise. So, new plan."

Grady holstered his weapon, then without warning he dashed toward Tasha. Pete tried to intercept him, but one of the sharks lunged forward and grabbed his leg in its jaws. Pete bellowed in agony, and he turned toward the shark and started pounding its head with both fists while blood ran from his leg and pooled on the ground around his feet.

Jarrod stepped in front of Tasha to protect her, but Grady was a younger – and beefier – man. He backhanded Jarrod across the face, and the actor stumbled to the side. He would've gone down if he hadn't managed to slap his hands against the alley wall to steady himself.

Grady grabbed Tasha and wrapped his arms around her tight. Shari started kicking the shark that had sunk its teeth into her husband's leg, and Tamara ran toward Grady, hoping to somehow free Tasha. But before she could reach them, the umbilicus attached to Grady's spine drew taut, and the man was yanked violently off his feet – and Tasha went with him. They flew through the air twenty feet before Grady landed hard on his back with the *crack* of breaking bones. The man didn't cry out in pain from his injuries, nor did he loosen his grip on Tasha. The umbilicus retracted rapidly, pulling Grady and Tasha toward one end of the alley. Grady's body slid across the ground as if it was slick as ice, and then he and Tasha disappeared into the night.

The four landsharks that had answered Inez's summons remained motionless, and Jarrod wondered if Inez was so focused on bringing Tasha to her – where she was physically located – that she'd forgotten about the sharks, and in the absence of direct orders, the creatures just sat there, waiting.

"The weapons," Jarrod said.

Everyone had been watching Grady being recalled by the Mass, as motionless as the four sharks. Pete couldn't move because one of the creatures still maintained its grip on his leg, but Susan and Tamara sprang into action. The women dashed forward, Susan grabbing the shotgun and Tamara picking up the machete. Susan raised her gun and fired at one of the sharks. As its head exploded – painting the alley walls crimson – Tamara tossed the machete to Pete. The man had to have been in agony from his wound, but he caught the machete easily, then jammed the point into one of the shark's crimson eyes, shoving until the blade sank deep.

Pete might not have been an especially admirable person in Jarrod's view, but the man was tough as hell, Jarrod had to give him that. Blood dribbled from the shark's wounded head, spilling from its ruined socket and dribbling from its mouth, mixing with Pete's own blood. Pete gritted his teeth and yanked the machete free. The shark slumped to the ground, but its grip on Pete's leg didn't slacken.

While Pete contended with his shark, Susan was busy dealing with the remaining three. She'd already killed one, and the remaining two – their survival instincts kicking into gear – began moving again. They lunged toward her, jaws open wide. She blasted one in the mouth, knocking it backward, but the other kept coming. Pete tossed the machete to Shari, and she began hacking at its umbilicus. The last shark whirled on Shari the moment she began trying to sever its cord, but Susan stepped forward, lowered the shotgun's barrel to its head and fired. Blood and meat splattered Shari, and she closed her mouth and eyes, shivering with disgust.

Everyone looked around, expecting to see hordes of landsharks rushing toward them from both directions. But aside from them, and the four dead sharks, the alley remained empty.

"Help me get this fucker off my leg," Pete said. His voice was strained, and Jarrod knew the man was in far more pain than he was letting on.

Working together, Jarrod, Susan, Shari, and Tamara worked on freeing Pete. Jarrod and Susan pried open the jaws – being careful not to slice their hands on the animal's teeth – while Tamara and Shari grabbed hold of its tail and pulled. The women only managed to move it a couple inches, but that was enough. Pete took in a hissing breath as the shark's teeth disengaged from his flesh. The wounds had already been bleeding, but without the teeth plugging the holes, blood flowed more freely, and Pete's pants leg became soaked with it.

Jarrod and Susan released the shark's mouth, and Jarrod quickly removed his belt, bent down, and wrapped it around Pete's leg above where his injuries were. He threaded the leather strap through the buckle and tightened it. Pete drew in a sharp breath, and when Jarrod finished making the belt secure, he stood once more. Jarrod swayed on his feet, a bit dizzy, but the sensation quickly passed. So far, his cancer-ravaged body was holding up, but he didn't know how much more exertion it could take before it refused to go any further.

Tamara removed her shirt. She wasn't wearing a bra, but she displayed no sign of self-consciousness. Why would she? Pete and Shari had seen her breasts before, and Jarrod was gay. She ripped her shirt down the back, then knelt and tied it around Pete's leg as a makeshift bandage. Jarrod wasn't certain this was necessary since Pete's leg was already tied off with a tourniquet, but he figured it couldn't hurt. Shari and Tamara took up positions on either side of Pete to support him. He gratefully put his arms around their shoulders and took his weight off his wounded leg.

"We need to go after Tasha," Jarrod said.

"We *need* to get Pete to a hospital," Tamara countered.

They all looked at each other for several moments without speaking. Jarrod wanted to yell at Tamara, demand to know how she could even contemplate abandoning Tasha. But then he reminded himself that despite what Inez had said, this wasn't a movie. Heroes didn't shrug off wounds that would fell ordinary mortals and keep forging onward. If Pete didn't get medical attention soon, there was a good chance he'd bleed out, tourniquet or no tourniquet. And in his current condition, he wouldn't be much help on any rescue mission they might mount. Jarrod knew Shari and Tamara wouldn't leave Pete. Somewhere along the line tonight they'd become a trio – even if they hadn't realized it yet.

He gave Susan a questioning look. She didn't really know Tasha, didn't really know any of them, for that matter, and he had no right to ask her to risk her life any further. But Tasha needed help, and he knew he couldn't give it to her alone. Susan held his gaze for a moment, her expression unreadable. Then she gave him a grim smile.

"If we're going to do this, we'd better get moving," she said.

"Thank you." Jarrod turned to the others. "Good luck."

"Same to you," Pete said.

Shari and Tamara gave him farewell smiles, and then the three of them started making their way to one end of the alley, while Jarrod and Susan started toward the other.

* * * * *

The air was squeezed from Tasha's lungs as she was yanked backward along with Grady, who was really Inez who was really the Mass. And when Grady hit the ground, the jolt was enough to render her temporarily unconscious. When she came to, she was looking up at a starlit night sky, the almost-full moon painting the world with soft silver light. At first she didn't understand why the stars were moving. She knew they appeared to be in motion as the Earth revolved and rotated around the sun, but she couldn't remember them ever moving so *fast*. Then she realized the stars weren't moving. She was.

Adrenaline shot through her, instantly clearing her mind. She remembered everything about this batshit-crazy night, and the most insane thing about it so far – that the Mass had captured her and was planning to literally drag her out to sea. She chided herself for being foolish enough to attempt to probe the Mass' mind using Grady as a conduit. It hadn't occurred to her that the Mass would be able to sense what she was doing. All her life she'd thought of psychic powers as something belonging to the world of the future, a sign of advancing human evolution, and not as an ability that an ancient, supposedly primitive, being might possess. But it made sense. The Mass remained in constant contact with the minds of its Hunters, so when Tasha connected psychically with one of them, she was connecting to the Mass as well. And once the Mass had sensed her intrusion into its mind, it decided a closer look at her was in order. She considered resuming her mental probe of the Mass, but she wasn't sure it was a good idea. If the Mass decided she was a threat, it would kill her. If she wanted to stay alive, she needed to remain an interesting – but ultimately harmless – curiosity.

The ride through Sailor's Walk was not a smooth one. Grady bounced and juddered across the cobblestones, and the constant impacts made Tasha's body ache, and she soon began to develop a fierce headache. This latter effect could be due, at least in part, to her recent psychic exertions. She'd never exercised her abilities as much as she had this night and never to such a degree. So she was unable to do more than go along for the ride and endure the bumping and jostling as best she could.

Eventually they left Sailor's Walk and its cobblestone streets, and the ride smoothed out some after that. They passed a number of landsharks. Most of them were either carrying severed body parts to the Mass or, having already delivered their loads, had returned to the land in search of more. She saw few people and fewer vehicles, but she heard shouts and screams, footfalls as people ran, tires screeching. It seemed plenty of prey remained in the area for the Hunters to chase. She prayed the people would escape, knowing that too many of them wouldn't.

Before too much longer, Grady's body slid off the pavement and onto the sand. Tasha smelled saltwater and heard the *shhushh* of surf, and she knew they were nearing the ocean. Grady's grip continued being as strong as ever, but the man – or Inez – hadn't said a word since they'd left the alley, and she wondered if he *could* speak now. Being dragged across the ground so far and so fast had to have torn the shit out of Grady's back, legs, and ass. How badly was he hurt? Could the Mass continue exerting control over his body if he was unconscious, or even dead? Maybe.

She tried to steal herself against the shock of entering the water, but it still took her by surprise. She swallowed saltwater, and it took all her control not to breathe it. But then Grady rose to the surface, and she was able to breathe safely. God, the water was cold! She began shivering, teeth clacking together, and she wondered if this was due to the emotional shock of the evening's events finally hitting her. But what did it matter? Either way, she was fucking freezing. The water gleamed with reflecting moonlight, and she saw dark fins gliding through the glow. They appeared to be keeping pace with Grady and her, although none came closer than ten feet. This suited her just fine.

She continued looking up at the night sky as they traveled farther out to sea. But they hadn't gone far before she felt a malevolent presence drawing closer. Or rather, *she* was drawing closer to *it*. She craned her head to look behind her so she could see what they were approaching. At first it looked like an island, but as she got closer the stench hit her – saltwater mixed with congealed blood and rotting meat. She knew then that what she saw wasn't an island but rather a living thing.

The Mass.

In the moonlight, it looked like a great mound of black rock, but when Grady was dragged up onto its surface, Tasha could feel the Mass give beneath their combined weight, as if it was semi-solid. The Mass stopped pulling Grady, and he came to a stop. For a moment he continued holding onto Tasha tightly, but then his grip relaxed, and his arms fell away from her. She immediately rolled off him, her body coming into contact with the Mass' surface for the first time. It was spongy and moist, and touching it made her feel queasy. The Mass bobbed gently in the water, but even this minimal movement made her nausea worse until she feared she was going to vomit. There was a breeze blowing, and the touch of it on her wet skin made her shiver.

Grady sat upright with a motion so sudden it made Tasha cry out in surprise. His face was expressionless, and when he looked at her, he did so without the slightest sign of recognition. He stood then and started walking back toward the water, moving stiffly. When he passed Tasha, she saw that his entire back – from the top of his head all the way down to his heels – was a ragged bloody ruin beneath the tatters of his uniform. He continued to the edge of the Mass, and when he reached the water, he threw himself in without hesitation. The water around him immediately began to churn and froth with violent activity, and Tasha could see the sleek dark shapes of sharks attacking Grady, biting into his flesh and tearing away great mouthfuls of meat.

Grady didn't make a single sound as he died.

Booze, bar food, and swallowed seawater spilled up out of Tasha's gut then, hot and acidic, and she leaned forward and emptied her stomach onto the Mass' corrugated surface.

It's like a scab, she thought. *Only one the size of a football field.*

She heard Inez's voice in her mind then.

Sorry you had to see that, but I'm a big believer in recycling. And since Grady wouldn't have survived his injuries much longer anyway, it was time he served me another way.

Tasha wiped her mouth with the back of her hand and then pushed herself into a sitting position. She felt weak and more than a little woozy, but at least she didn't feel like she had to throw up anymore.

"You mean as food," she said.

Yes.

An image flashed through her mind then, the sharks carrying pieces of Grady to the underside of the Mass where orifices opened to suck the sustenance in. It was a sickening sight, and she was doubly thankful that she'd already thrown up everything that had been in her stomach. As it was, she still had a couple of dry heaves.

You're a remarkable girl, Inez said. *More than you probably imagine. You might very well possess the most highly developed mind on the planet.* She paused, then added, *On land, anyway.*

"You're not Inez," she said. "Inez is dead. You've just put her on like a mask. But the real you is still underneath."

Perhaps. But if I've absorbed the chemicals and electrical impulses that made up the consciousness called Inez, then she's not truly dead, is she?

Tasha didn't have time for existential arguments with a prehistoric sea monster.

"Call your Hunters back, all of them," she said. "You don't need to hurt anyone else. You've got me and you've fed well tonight. Why not just head on out to sea once more and forget humans ever existed?"

You're trying to protect your friends. At least the ones that are still alive. How touching. I didn't bring you here to critique how I'm managing this production. I brought you here because I want to have a heart-to-heart talk with you – about your future.

Tasha felt the part of the Mass she was sitting on soften beneath her, become almost liquidy, and then an orifice yawned open and before she could do anything to prevent it, she fell inside. A moment later, the orifice closed, and the Mass continued bobbing gently in the water, as placid and serene as it had been since before the first dinosaur had trod the Earth.

Everything was going – Inez almost couldn't bring herself to think the pun – *swimmingly.*

CHAPTER TWELVE

"We need to find a car," Tamara said.

The three of them made their way down the sidewalk, moving as fast as they could given Pete's injury, which wasn't very. Tamara – holding the machete – was on Pete's left, Shari on his right, and all three kept watch for landsharks. The street was clear, for the moment, but Tamara wasn't foolish enough to believe it would stay that way. They needed a vehicle not only to get Pete to a hospital, but also to get them far enough away from the ocean that the sharks would no longer be a threat. There were numerous signs that they hadn't been the only ones who'd had to deal with the sharks tonight. There were smears of blood on the sidewalks and streets, along with the occasional severed hand or shoe with a foot still in it. Storefront windows had been shattered, cars had hit lampposts, buildings, and other cars, and several vehicles had simply been abandoned, their drivers nowhere to be seen. Maybe some of them had managed to escape with their lives, but if so, Tamara didn't think the number of survivors was very high.

Pete surprised Tamara then by laughing.

"Can you believe this shit?" he said. "I knew Inez could be something of a monster, but this is extreme even for her."

Tamara couldn't help laughing at that herself, and Shari joined in.

When they finished laughing, Shari said, "When we get back to LA, maybe we could, you know . . ."

"What?" Tamara asked.

"Stay together," Shari finished. "The three of us."

That took Tamara by surprise. It hadn't been that long ago that Shari and Pete had been pissed to learn that she'd been fucking them both. Now Shari wanted her to shack up with them?

"I'd like that," Pete said. "And not just because of the sex. Although don't get me wrong, that part would be great. We just seem to kind of, well, *fit*."

Tamara knew what Pete meant. Somewhere along the line tonight they'd gone from being an extremely uncomfortable love triangle to a cooperative – and complementary – trio. She had plans for her career, though. Big ones. And she wasn't sure she wanted to be tied down to any one person, or in this case, two persons. Still, it *could* be fun . . .

"Let's worry about that later," Tamara said. "After we get Pete fixed up." She looked at Shari. "Can you hold him up by yourself for a minute? I want to see if any of those abandoned cars have keys in them." *And if they're still driveable*, she thought.

"Hey, I don't need help to stand," Pete protested. But his voice indicated otherwise. It was weak and breathy. He'd lost a significant amount of blood when the shark bit him, and while he was healthy as a fucking horse – as Tamara knew from their time in bed – even a strong, fit body could only take so much punishment.

"I got him," Shari said.

Tamara insisted Shari take the machete, and then she smiled at them both and headed into the street. She hoped Jarrod and Susan would succeed in rescuing Tasha, but she knew odds were that they'd be shark food before they reached the ocean. Still, she admired their bravery. It seemed Jarrod had more than a little real-life hero in him. It was a damn shame about his cancer, but at least if a shark *did* get him, he'd die knowing he wouldn't have lived much longer anyway. Cold comfort, perhaps, but it was something.

The first car Tamara tried – a Ford Taurus – had an automatic ignition, but without a key, there was no way to start it. The windshield had been broken out, by sharks no doubt, and it would be no protection if any of the fuckers came at them. But the second vehicle – a Jeep Renegade – had smashed into the side of a seafood restaurant called Cappy's on the other side of the street from where Shari and Pete stood. The vehicle didn't appear to have sustained enough damage in the collision to render it inoperable. Its driver's side door hung open and when Tamara jogged over to the vehicle, she saw a pair of jean-clad legs attached to a trunk sitting behind the wheel. There was no sign of the top half of the body, and Tamara wasn't certain if it had been male or female. She supposed it didn't matter. Everyone was equal in death's eyes. There was a shitload of blood, of course, soaking the seat and floor, and splattered on the inside of the windshield. Bitten-off ends of intestine protruded from the trunk, and the sight of the viscera made her feel queasy. But when she glanced at the ignition, she was happy to see keys dangling from it. What had turned out to be a really shitty night so far had just taken a 180 degree turn for the better.

She turned back toward Shari and Pete and waved to catch their attention, and when they looked at her she gave them a thumbs up. They started toward her, Pete leaning on Shari and hopping on one foot, and Tamara turned back to the vehicle. The driver's seatbelt was buckled, but since the body's top half was gone, there was nothing for the belt to hold onto. The legs were skinny, and she didn't think she'd have much trouble pulling them out. She didn't want to touch the grisly jeans, but if she wanted to drive the Jeep, she would have to get her hands dirty. She grabbed hold of a couple of the dead person's belt loops and pulled. The half body came out of the seat easily enough, tipped toward Tamara, and spilled what remained of its guts onto her feet as it fell. She let out a cry of disgust and skipped backward. The trunk and legs hit the asphalt and lay there, coils of intestine slowly oozing outward, as if she was watching a slow-motion anatomy film. Feeling queasier than ever, she examined the driver's seat. It was covered with blood, so whoever drove it would have to sit in that shit as they made their escape.

Fine with me, she thought. It was a lot better than having to sit in your own blood.

Tamara had been in a half dozen cheap horror movies, all of them literally dripping with gore. She'd seen human heads and limbs get chopped off, watched someone being stabbed multiple times, saw innocent people torn apart. All of it fake, of course, but she'd thought these experiences might've hardened her to the effects of real violence. But as it turned out, her past self hadn't known shit. Looking back now, all those special effects looked like the efforts of kids making their own amateur horror videos. She thought those effects were made to look fake on purpose, to insulate audiences, protect them from thinking they were seeing the real thing. If she managed to survive this night, she vowed never to make another goddamned horror film again.

She turned around to face Shari and Pete. They were halfway across the street when three landsharks came trundling around the corner. Tamara didn't know if her cry of surprise had alerted them, if they'd smelled the guts spilling out of the half-a-body she'd just dumped onto the street, or if they somehow sensed Pete's vulnerability and were attracted to it. Really, what the fuck did it matter why the goddamned things were coming? All that mattered was they were.

"Get in the car!" she shouted. "Hurry!"

She slid into the Jeep's driver's seat – *slid* being the operative word with all the blood – shut the door, and turned the key in the ignition.

Work, you bastard! she thought.

The engine roared to life and Tamara threw the vehicle into reverse. The Jeep's front end was damaged and the steering wheel didn't want to turn all the way, but she managed to back the vehicle into the street and swing it around until it pointed at Pete and Shari. The sharks were still coming toward them, but Pete and Shari had stopped in the middle of the street, and it looked like they were . . . *arguing* with each other? Pete was trying to push Shari away from him – nearly losing his balance – but Shari stubbornly remained where she was.

He wants her to leave him, doesn't want to slow her down and get her killed. But she won't go, no matter how much he wants her to. She won't abandon him.

At that moment she felt something very much like love for the two of them.

But their arguing had cost them precious moments, and the sharks were almost upon them. There was nothing Tamara could do to save them. She had no weapons. Shari and Pete had the machete, but it wouldn't be enough to stop three sharks attacking simultaneously. And Shari and Pete stood between her and the sharks, so she couldn't attempt to run the monsters over with the Jeep. Pete and Shari – her beautiful lovers – were going to die. Nothing she could do would prevent that.

She took her foot off the brake and jammed it down on the accelerator. The Jeep surged forward and Tamara aimed the vehicle at Pete and Shari. Her vision blurred as tears filled her eyes, but she thought she saw Pete and Shari look at her just as the sharks fell upon them. She closed her eyes just before the impact.

The Jeep kept going until it slammed into the front of a tattoo parlor across the street called Inkstained. The engine died, and Tamara sat there, gripping the steering wheel so tight her hands throbbed, tears streaming down her face. Were Pete and Shari dead? God, she hoped so. But what if she hadn't hit them hard enough to kill them – or the sharks? What if they were still alive but horribly injured? They could be suffering terribly, and it would be all her fault.

She pulled her hands from the wheel, opened the door and got out of the Jeep. She turned and started walking into the street, then stopped and stared. Shari and Pete's bodies lay in a twisted, bloody heap along with those of three equally bloody and dead sharks. And rooting around in the carnage, happy as a pig in slop, was a fourth shark, this one very much alive. It was taking huge mouthfuls of both human and shark meat and gulping them down with enthusiasm. She didn't know where it had come from. Maybe she'd missed it when she saw the other three approaching. Maybe it had come upon the scene from a different direction, drawn by the noise and blood. She wished she had the machete, but Shari had been holding it when the Jeep hit her. No way Tamara could get it now.

She didn't want to abandon her lovers, but there was nothing she could do for them now. She could mourn them later. Right now she needed to get the fuck out of there. Keeping her eyes on the fourth shark the entire time, she began slowly moving down the street, in a direction she hoped would lead her further inland. She got less than ten feet before the fourth shark turned its head toward her. It didn't hesitate. The instant it saw her, it started toward her, scuttling across asphalt on its insect-like legs, moving almost as fast as it could in water, umbilicus trailing behind it.

Tamara turned to run –

– and her left ankle twisted. A sharp bolt of pain, and the leg gave out on her. She went down hard, her left hip and elbow hitting asphalt. The pain in her elbow was especially bad, and she wondered if she'd broken the damn thing. She didn't have time to worry about that, though. She pushed herself up onto her ass and turned around to see the shark coming at her, jaws opening and closing in an almost mechanical fashion, as if the thing wasn't real, was nothing more than something Enrique had put together in his shop. Except this special effect was about to kill her.

She didn't bother trying to crab walk backward to try and escape. There was no point. She knew she wouldn't make it. She squeezed her eyes shut tight and waited for death to claim her.

And waited.

She could hear the shark's mouth working, could even hear the whiskery sound of the cilia on its underside trying to propel it forward. She could even *smell* the goddamned thing. But she did not feel its teeth sinking into her flesh.

She risked opening her eyes.

The shark was less than three feet away from her, but although it strained forward, teeth gnashing as it tried to get its mouth on her, it moved no closer. At first she was at a loss as to why this was happening, and then she saw the umbilicus protruding from behind the shark's second dorsal fin had been pulled taut. She burst out laughing.

"You ran out of leash, didn't you, you fucker?"

From the moment the landsharks had attacked Flotsam, it seemed the creature's umbilical cords could stretch endlessly. But long as they might be, they still had limits, as she now witnessed. The shark thrashed, whipping its body back and forth, hundreds of tiny feet scrabbling furiously in a vain attempt to move forward, gill fronds pulsing. If only Pete and Shari had reached this point before the sharks attacked. If they had, her lovers would still be alive and all three of them would be well on their way to a hospital. The shark fixed its crimson-eyed stare on her, and although the creature possessed no real intelligence, she could've sworn the thing was glaring at her in frustration. She smiled savagely at the struggling animal.

"Fuck you," she spat.

Then the barbed end of the shark's umbilicus tore free in a spray of saltwater mixed with blood. No longer bound by the umbilicus, the shark surged toward Tamara. Without its umbilicus, the shark would die. The creature didn't know that, though. Or if it did, it didn't care. Just so long as it got to kill her first.

She'd always believed that intense pleasure and intense pain were simply two sides of the same coin – absolute, overwhelming sensation – and she believed it was possible to experience pain so great it was indistinguishable from pleasure.

She was about to find out.

She'd had so many plans for her career. Better roles in larger, more high-profile productions. Higher salaries, maybe even an award or two. But none of it was going to happen now, and the biggest surprise to her was how little she cared.

When the dying shark got its teeth into her, she discovered that intense pleasure and pain were definitely *not* the same.

Not even close.

* * * * *

Jarrod had done a lot of things in his acting career but driving a police cruiser was a first. Susan literally rode shotgun, holding tight to her weapon and scanning the streets for any sign of sharks as they drove. She also navigated, guiding him toward the ocean. They had the vehicle's emergency lights going in case they ran into other traffic, but the streets were mostly clear. They passed other abandoned police cruisers and an empty EMS vehicle. It was no mystery what had happened to their drivers. They'd responded to emergency calls about landsharks attacking only to end up dead themselves.

Jarrod and Susan had come across Grady's abandoned cruiser not long after parting ways with Tamara, Pete, and Shari. The driver's door had been open, and the engine still running, as if the vehicle had been waiting for them. Jarrod drove as fast as he could, running through red lights and taking turns so sharply the cruiser's tires squealed in protest. He didn't know what Inez – the *Mass* – intended to do with Tasha, but whatever it was, it couldn't be good, and he knew time wasn't on their side. They needed to get to Tasha as fast as they could, and they had a plan, basic though it was. From what Tasha had said, the Mass was in the ocean, close to shore mostly likely, so its Hunters could reach as far inland as possible.

That meant they needed a boat. Susan had lived in Bridgewater all her life, and while she didn't own a boat of her own, she knew where to find one. There was a boat rental place on the beach where people could rent small craft with outboard motors for fishing or joyriding. As for what Susan and he would do when they found the Mass . . . well, Jarrod was still working on that.

He was grateful for Susan's help, but he was having second thoughts about her joining him on this rescue mission. It was one thing for him to risk his life. He was already dying. But Susan was young and healthy. She had everything to lose and nothing to gain by helping him.

"Susan, once I get a boat, you don't need –"

"Hush," Susan said, not unkindly. "This isn't something you can do yourself, not in . . ." She trailed off.

"My condition?" Jarrod said.

Susan said nothing.

Jarrod wanted to tell her she was being insulting, but he knew she was right. It had become harder for him to do regular day-to-day activities over the last few weeks, and he had no idea how long his body would hold up under the kind of strain he was putting on it tonight. He was an old, dying man. Not exactly action-hero material. But his leukemia gave him an advantage most people didn't have. He wasn't afraid to die, and when you didn't fear death, you could do anything.

"Take a left up ahead," Susan said, and he did so.

On one hand, it was a relief that they hadn't encountered any more landsharks during their drive, but it was also worrying. Jarrod feared the Mass might've recalled its Hunters to the water, and if that was the case, it might then head back out to sea. It would be hard enough to find the creature at night, even with the moonlight to aid them, but if the goddamned thing submerged, they'd have no chance.

If it submerges, Tasha will drown, he thought, and their rescue mission would be over before it began. All the more reason to get to the boat rental place as fast as they could.

"Not that I'm ungrateful for your assistance," Jarrod began.

"But why am I risking my life to help you and Tasha?"

He nodded.

"Would you believe me if I said because it's the right thing to do?"

"There's a big difference between the right thing and a suicide mission," Jarrod said.

Susan laughed.

"True enough. I guess I couldn't let you go by yourself. Everybody needs backup, right? Besides, those fucking sharks tore the shit out of my bar and killed my customers. And to be honest, I never really liked Inez."

Now it was Jarrod's turn to laugh.

They reached the beach soon after that. Jarrod drove the cruiser onto the sand and pulled right up to the boat rental place, which was called, imaginatively enough, *Boat Rentals*. The cruiser's emergency lights were still flashing, and he wondered if he should turn them off so as to not warn Inez they were coming. He decided it didn't matter. Inez *wanted* them to come to her. Their rescue attempt was going to be the climactic scene in the "movie" her deranged mind had envisioned. He wasn't sure what had happened to Inez, but it was clear that she'd somehow joined with the Mass, that her consciousness had blended with its. He wondered if Inez still lived or if the Mass had only adopted her thought patterns? If she lived, maybe there was a possibility she could be saved, too. If so, it would probably be a long shot at best, but if there was a chance, regardless of how slight it might be, Jarrod would take it.

Susan walked to the side door of the building – really little more than a brick shack – and told Jarrod to step back. She pounded the butt of the shotgun against the wood next to the doorknob three times before the lock broke and the door swung inward. She handed the shotgun to Jarrod, who almost dropped it, and then she went inside. It had been some time since he'd fired a gun, back when he was preparing for a role as a hit man in a crime thriller titled *Kill Me Twice*. He'd learned to shoot pistols, rifles, and shotguns then, but that had been almost twenty years ago. Still, he felt confident that he remembered the basics. He raised the gun to his shoulder and guarded the entrance while Susan did whatever she was doing.

He thought of Tamara, Shari, and Pete then. He hoped they'd made it out of Sailor's Walk and managed to find medical care for Pete. He supposed there was an excellent chance he would never know. All he could do was hope for the best. In the end, wasn't that all anyone could do?

When Susan came out of the building a moment later, she was holding an ignition key. A number dangled from it, printed with black marker on a round white piece of plastic. Number 6. Susan took back the shotgun, handed Jarrod the key, and they headed for the small dock where the boats were moored. Susan held her shotgun at the ready, scanning the beach for any sign of landshark activity, but there was none.

The craft consisted of skiffs and what Susan said were bay boats, the latter designed for use close to shore. The bay boats were made of fiberglass and measured around twenty feet in length. Most importantly, they didn't look too difficult to pilot. The boat numbers were painted on the boards of the dock, so finding Number 6 was no hard task. Jarrod got in first, and Susan untied the mooring line, tossed it into the boat, and then joined Jarrod. Before starting the boat, she reached into her pants pocket, removed a small object, and placed it into his hand. It was a matchbook which said *Flotsam* on the cover, along with the bar's address and phone number.

"You can't smoke in bars or restaurants in Bridgewater," she said, "but matchbooks are still good advertisements. I always keep a few on me."

"Why are you giving this to me?" Jarrod asked. "Nothing personal, but if I live through tonight, I'm not going to want a souvenir to remember it by."

She smiled and hooked a thumb aft.

"There should be a fuel container back there. I only have a handful of shells left, and we might need to improvise a weapon when we reach the Mass."

"Good thinking," Jarrod said.

Susan grinned. "Only kind I do." She nodded to the boat's steering console. "You want to pilot this thing or do you want to shoot at sharks?"

"You've been doing fine in the shooting department this evening, and I've piloted watercraft of various kinds before."

"Aye, aye Captain Drayton."

Jarrod went to the boat's console, inserted the key into the ignition switch, and turned it. The engine activated with a rumble, loud and strong. Jarrod stood at the console, and Susan took up a position in the bow ahead of him. He put the motor in reverse, making sure to go gentle on the throttle. The craft backed out of the slip, then Jarrod put the engine in drive and gave it a little more throttle. The bay boat started moving forward, slowly at first, but as soon as they'd gotten past the dock, he gave it more speed.

"It's a beautiful night to go monster hunting," Susan said.

It was an odd thought, but Jarrod couldn't disagree with it. The sky was clear, the moon was shining bright, and the ocean was calm and smooth as glass. Too bad they weren't really making a film. The conditions were perfect for a night shoot.

"Now all we have to do is find the Mass," Susan said. "Any idea where to look?"

"Tasha said she sensed it earlier today, when we were filming on the beach. I say we start there."

"Good a place as any," Susan said. "Head east." She pointed, and Jarrod turned the craft in that direction and shoved the throttle forward as far as it would go.

CHAPTER THIRTEEN

Tasha returned to consciousness in darkness. At first she thought she'd awakened in the middle of the night, and she intended to roll over and return to sleep. But when she tried to move, nothing happened. Confused, she tried to wiggle her fingers and toes, but again, nothing happened. At least, she didn't *feel* anything happening. Was she sick or injured? Was she in a coma? Panic overwhelmed her, and she tried crying out for someone, anyone to help, but no sound emerged from her throat. She was alone. Absolutely, utterly alone.

I wouldn't go that far, dear.

The voice startled Tasha. It felt strange, as if she wasn't hearing it so much as *experiencing* it.

You've never mentally communicated with a mind as strong as yours before, have you? Inez said. *It must be strange for you to hear another thought-voice.*

Rather than relieving her panic, hearing Inez's voice only made it worse.

"Where am I? What happened to me?"

Where you're at is a simple question to answer. You're inside the Mass, floating in Bridgewater Bay about a half mile from shore. We moved out here so Jarrod would have a final journey to make – much more dramatic that way. But we didn't go too far. As ill as the poor thing is, we don't want to overtax him.

Now that Tasha was in direct telepathic communication with Inez/the Mass, she was getting a better idea of the intelligence she was dealing with. As she'd sensed before, it was ancient and powerful, but it hadn't been self-aware, at least not in the way humans thought of the concept. Inez wasn't the first human the Mass had ever absorbed, but she was the most imaginative. The Mass had been intrigued by her imagination, so it had, in essence, downloaded her mind and was using it like an operating system. But because Inez produced films for a living, the Mass – not fully understanding the abstract concept of a movie – had attempted to make one of its own. It was, for the first time in its unbelievably long life, exploring creativity. Everything that had happened tonight, every life that had been lost, all the blood that had been spilled, had all been part of the Mass' first production.

I'm thinking of calling it Blood Island. *Simple but impactful, yes? What do you think of my movie so far? Be honest now. I can take it.*

Good god. The fucking thing was asking her for story notes? She ignored the question and repeated one of her own.

"What happened to me?"

That's difficult to explain. It might be easier if I showed you.

A cascade of information flooded Tasha's mind, complex biological data mixed with physical sensations. When it was over, she understood what had been done to her, and she was horrified. Her body was gone, absorbed by the Mass. Only her brain remained, housed within its substance – a literal island of blood – and connected directly to its nervous system, just as had been done with Inez's mind.

"You killed me!"

Within me, you'll live until the end of time. I haven't killed you. I've made you immortal. I'm sure you'll adjust to your new reality in a century or two, but right now we need to get ready for the final act of our little drama. Jarrod is coming.

Tasha felt the departure of Inez's mental presence, and although she called out to the woman and demanded she return and talk further, she received no reply.

She understood the Mass was using her as a lure to bring Jarrod to it, and sweet, brave idiot that he was, he'd fallen for it. She knew the Mass had no intention of allowing Jarrod to be victorious. The creature might be following the paradigm of a monster movie, but it was never going to allow the hero to defeat it. Jarrod would die – sooner than he had to – and it was all because of her. The Mass' curiosity about the lifeforms on shore had been peaked when their two minds had briefly touched earlier in the day. If she hadn't been on the shore with the rest of the film crew, the Mass would've eaten its fill of sea life in the area and eventually moved on, just as if had for millions of years. Before, it had been nothing more than an animal, an amazing prehistoric survivor like those pliosaurs in the waters around the South-American island of *Las Dagas*. But with the addition of Inez's mind, it had become a monster.

She had to do something to help Jarrod stop the Mass. But what? All that remained of her was her mind. But hers was far from a normal mind, wasn't it? She was a telepath, a strong one. The Mass had left her with her most potent weapon intact, *and* it had put her inside it. Two very big mistakes, ones Tasha hoped would prove fatal.

She relaxed her mind, allowed her thoughts to quiet, and when she was ready, she went to work.

* * * * *

Finding the Mass turned out to be far simpler than Jarrod anticipated. They'd only been traveling for several minutes before the first shark fin broke the surface. It was quickly followed by several more, and Jarrod feared that Susan and he were about to be attacked. But instead of coming at the boat, the sharks lined up in a single file and began swimming out to sea.

"What are they doing?" Susan asked.

Jarrod let out a bitter laugh.

"Inez wants to make sure we find the Mass, so she's sent some of her pets to guide us." He didn't know whether to be relieved or insulted. Did Inez think he was so far past his prime that he couldn't locate one fucking sea monster hanging around the bay? But something else about the escort disturbed him more. It was a display of Inez's control. *She* was in charge of this production, and she intended for it to go precisely according to plan. *Her* plan. Susan and he were doing exactly what Inez wanted, and if they continued playing the roles she'd created for them, how could they hope to defeat her? He could see no other option, though, so he followed the sharks.

"What do you think the Mass *is* exactly?" Susan asked.

"I don't know. From its name, I assume it's big. And the word conjures up images of nasty growths inside the body. Horrid, shapeless things that might or might not kill you."

"Like cancer," Susan said.

"The irony isn't lost on me," Jarrod said wryly.

They continued following the sharks for several minutes until they saw a large dark shape ahead of them. At first, Jarrod thought it was an island, but he didn't remember there being one in the bay. But when the shark fins slid beneath the surface, he understood that they had reached their destination. This was the Mass. He throttled back and allowed the boat to slow. It drifted toward the Mass, and when a wave threatened to push it further away, a shark appeared and bumped into the craft's hull, nudging it back toward the Mass. The boat's prow struck the Mass with a soft *chuk* and held fast, almost as if the Mass had grabbed hold of it. Jarrod cut the engine, and Susan disembarked first. She then helped him onto the surface of the Mass. It gave beneath their feet as if they were standing on flesh, but the surface was craggy, like rock. Jarrod knelt to touch it and found it was as rough as it looked. It was like touching a gigantic scab. He scratched at the surface, and when he examined his finger, he saw dark liquid on it. He sniffed and detected the distinct odor of blood. He stood and wiped his finger on the side of his pants.

He looked around, but even with the moonlight to see by, he couldn't tell how large the Mass was. Big as a whale, he thought. Maybe bigger.

He called out for Tasha.

"Tasha! Can you hear me? It's Jarrod! Are you here? Are you hurt?"

The only sound that came in response was the water lapping at the Mass' edge.

Jarrod looked up. No seagulls. He thought the birds would've been attracted to the Mass' organic matter, but then he realized that any gulls – or any other creature – foolish enough to come near the Mass would be absorbed. And Susan and he were standing on its surface.

"This is a bad idea," Jarrod said. "We need to get back in –"

The Mass released its grip on the bay boat, and the craft began to drift away. Jarrod thought they could swim for it, but then crimson-threaded fins broke the surface and began patrolling the water between the Mass and the boat – which still held the fuel container they'd planned to use as a weapon.

"Too late," Susan said. "What's wrong? Getting cold feet? Not that I'd blame you. This is scary as fuck."

"I just realized we're standing on top of a creature that's like a gigantic amoeba. It can absorb whatever it wants."

Susan looked down at the surface of the Mass, her eyes widening in terror. "Shit! Why did you *tell* me that? There's a reason they say ignorance is bliss."

Jarrod couldn't argue with that.

"Let's start looking for Tasha," he said. "That's why Inez brought us here – to attempt her rescue – and I don't think Inez will kill us before we reach the climax of the story she's telling herself." Not a comforting thought, perhaps, but it was all he had to offer. Susan evidently didn't have anything better to say, for she remained silent.

They began slowly making their way across the Mass, walking side by side. The surface was rough and difficult to navigate. There were numerous cracks and crevices in the creature's outer hide – could you call it skin? – and it would be only too easy to take a wrong step, get your foot caught in a crack, and break your ankle. Jarrod didn't know how long they walked or how much distance they traveled. Without any sort of landmarks, it was difficult to tell, but eventually Susan pointed and said, "Look!"

Jarrod tried to see what she was pointing at, but even with the moon's light to aid his eyes, at first he didn't see it. After several seconds of staring in the direction Susan indicated, a lump on the Mass' hide, which he'd taken as another bit of the rough terrain that formed the creature's surface, resolved itself into the shape of a person lying down. A person who wasn't moving.

"Tasha!" Jarrod shouted. He headed toward her, moving as fast as he could without heed to where his feet came down. In the short time he'd known Tasha, she'd become a friend. An intimate one, as they'd literally shared thoughts. Risking a broken ankle was the least he could do for her. Susan followed as best she could, but Jarrod reached Tasha first and knelt beside her. He wanted to scoop her up into his arms, but he feared she might be injured, and he didn't want to cause her any further damage.

"Tasha? It's Jarrod. Can you hear me?" He repeated this last sentence in his mind. *Can you hear me?*

No response.

She was lying on her side, her back to them, and Jarrod reached out, took hold of her shoulder, and gave her a gentle shake. She rolled over – no, she flopped – onto her back, and when she did, Jarrod saw that her forehead was missing, as if the skin and bone had been eaten away by acid, and her skull was hollow. He cried out in horror and fell back on his ass. Tasha's dead eyes stared at him, almost glowing in the moonlight. Susan made thick gulping sounds as she fought to keep from throwing up.

"The Mass took Inez's mind," Jarrod said. "And it took Tasha's, too."

They were too late, but then, they were always meant to be too late, weren't they? In her twisted mind, Inez was making a horror movie. Jarrod and Susan never had a chance of rescuing Tasha. It wasn't in the script.

The area of the Mass beneath Tasha's body subsided, forming a depression which widened and opened into a hole. Tasha's body began to fall into it, and Jarrod reached for her out of some half-assed notion that he might at least be able to take her body back to land for a decent burial. But the hole sealed over and Jarrod's hand only struck the Mass' damp, spongy surface. Now that the goddamned creature had had its fun with Tasha's body, it was going to absorb her. In the wild, no animal ever wasted food.

Jarrod rose to his feet on legs that trembled from a combination of exhaustion and fury. He snatched the shotgun out of Susan's hand, turned away from her, worked the pump, shouldered the weapon, aimed it at the Mass' corrugated hide, and fired. Chunks of the Mass' gelatinous meat flew through the air, and Jarrod continued working the pump and firing, yelling wordlessly as he did so. He continued until all the rounds were spent, and he would've continued working the pump and pulling the trigger even then if Susan hadn't taken the gun from him.

His clothes, face, and hands were splattered with the Mass' liquidy substance, and he stared at the holes he'd made in the creature's surface.

"Fuck you," he said.

As he watched, the holes filled in until the damage Jarrod had caused was repaired. Jarrod didn't need to be telepathic to understand the Mass' message.

Fuck you, too.

Susan removed more shells from her pants pocket and began reloading the gun.

"I only have three rounds left." She said this in a non-accusatory tone, but Jarrod still felt like a fool. He'd wasted ammunition and hadn't hurt the Mass at all.

He heard sounds then, a chorus of *whssk-whssk-whssks*, coming from all around them. A moment later the sharks came into view, undulating across the Mass, umbilical cords stretching out behind them. In the silver moonlight, they looked surreal, like creatures ripped out of some fevered nightmare and plunked down in the real world. There were – he made a quick count – eleven of the things coming toward them. The sharks were still far enough apart that space remained between them, but their ranks were closing fast. If Susan and he didn't make a run for it now, they'd lose whatever small chance of escape they had. He was about to yell for Susan to start running, but before he could do so, his feet sank into the Mass. He kept sinking until he was almost in up to his knees, and then the Mass solidified around his legs, trapping him. He looked at Susan and saw the same thing had happened to her. No running for them, not now, not ever again.

The sharks kept coming. *Whssk-whssk-whssk-whssk-whssk . . .*

Jarrod struggled to pull his legs free, but it was no use. The Mass held him too tightly. He and Susan were less than three feet apart, but there was nothing they could do to help each other. They couldn't free themselves, and the shotgun didn't have enough ammunition to fend off eleven sharks. Anguish welled up inside Jarrod. He'd failed Tasha, and he'd failed Susan, too. She'd followed a dying man on a doomed quest, and now she was going to pay the price.

Susan looked at Jarrod and gave him a sad smile.

"Remember when I said I had three shells left? Turns out that's one more than we need. Goodbye, Jarrod. I always thought your movies were fun."

At first Jarrod had no idea what she was talking about, but then she worked the pump, turned the shotgun around, pressed the barrel against the soft flesh under her jaw, and pulled the trigger. Her head snapped back in an explosion of noise, and the top of her skull was blown off. Her body fell backward, bending at the knees, and she lay there, face reduced to ragged meat and shattered bone, except for her left eye which actually blinked several more times before falling still. Based on what Susan had said before pulling the trigger, she'd expected the shotgun to fall out of her hands and land where Jarrod could pick it up and use it on himself. But her hands retained their grip on the weapon in death, and there was no way he could reach it, not trapped like this.

You should've shot me before killing yourself, he thought, with no small measure of disappointment. Now he had no choice but to wait for the sharks to reach him and begin tearing mouthfuls of meat from his body. He hoped they'd be quick about it, but this was going to be the climax of Inez's "movie," and he knew she would milk his dying for all it was worth. His death would be messy, slow, and agonizing. He almost wished someone was filming this. It was going to be spectacular.

* * * * *

Deep inside the Mass, Tasha had finished preparing her mind and was ready to make her move.

So she did.

* * * * *

When the ring of sharks was about to close in on Jarrod, several rushed past him and attacked the others. Five sharks went after the other six, and they were not fucking around. Instead of trying to sink their teeth into their opponents' bodies, they went for their umbilical cords. They managed to get a couple, tearing them apart with ease. The sharks affected began thrashing about, their exertions growing weaker with each passing second. But the sharks that were under assault quickly moved to defend themselves, and a savage battle broke out, with Jarrod in the middle, trapped.

He felt the Mass' grip on his legs ease then, and he heard Tasha speaking in his mind.

"Go get the boat."

He understood what was happening. Tasha was attempting to wrest control of the Mass and Inez – or at least the part of the Mass that thought it was Inez – didn't intend to go down without a fight. But neither did he. He pulled himself free of the Mass one leg at a time, then he stood and started running. He had to dodge sharks, most of which were bleeding from battle injuries now, and try not to trip over their umbilical cords. One of his feet got stuck in a crevice and he went down, but he was far enough away from the fighting sharks that none of them noticed him fall. He rose to his feet once more and continued running, but more slowly this time.

He realized he had no idea in which direction he should run. Not only that, but the boat had likely drifted away from the Mass, maybe too far for him to easily spot it. How could he – And then he felt Tasha touch his mind, and he knew which direction to go in. He veered to the left and kept on running. His heart pounded and his head felt light, and he was having difficulty catching his breath. Dark spots danced in his vision, and he thought how ironic it would be if he dropped dead from a heart attack now. Still, he continued onward.

He kept an eye out for sharks, but none appeared. He didn't know how many Hunters the Mass possessed, and of those, how many had died during the assault on Bridgewater. But however many remained, it seemed they were all busy, and his progress was unimpeded. When he reached the edge of the Mass, he almost ran right into the water, but he stopped himself. He saw the boat floating maybe fifty feet from the Mass. Not very far away at all, unless you were an old man with a cancer-ridden body who'd exerted himself more this night than he had in the entire last year. To Jarrod, that fifty feet might as well have been fifty miles. And while he saw no fins cutting the ocean's surface, he knew there was a chance some of the Mass' Hunters were swimming between him and the boat, waiting for him to be stupid enough to jump into the water.

Fuck it, he thought, and dove in.

The cold water shocked his system, giving him a much-needed jolt of adrenaline. He began swimming toward the boat with swift, strong strokes, but the energy burst was temporary and quickly faded, leaving him feeling heavy and slow. It would be so easy to stop swimming and allow himself to sink. Maybe a shark would get him or maybe he'd simply drown, but either way, it would be over. But he didn't give in to the temptation. Tasha was fighting hard to stop Inez, and he couldn't abandon her. And if Inez won and regained control of the entire Mass, she wouldn't stop killing. She'd do what any producer would once a film of theirs was complete: she'd start planning a sequel. He couldn't allow that to happen.

He forced himself to continue on, his arms and legs feeling heavy as stone. But he kept them moving, and after what seemed like hours but could only have been minutes, he reached the boat. He reached up and grabbed hold of the side, then hung there for a moment, trying to catch his breath. This would be the perfect opportunity for a shark to grab hold of his legs and pull him down into the depths where it would finish him off, most likely with the assistance of several of its friends. But he simply had to rest a bit before attempting to climb aboard. No sharp teeth sunk into his flesh, and he wasn't yanked beneath the surface. If any sharks remained in the water, they were probably fighting each other, just as the ones on the surface of the Mass were, which Jarrod figured was the only reason he remained alive. Tasha still had his back.

He hauled himself up and into the boat. The effort proved almost too much for him, and for an instant he blacked out, but his vision quickly cleared, and he was, if not in stellar shape, good to go. The fuel container was under the back seat, and Jarrod – wet, cold, and shivering in the night air – picked up the container, unscrewed the cap, tossed it aside, and began dumping gasoline onto the boat, splashing it randomly across the boat. He didn't worry overmuch about not getting any gas on himself. He wasn't intending to survive this next little trip. When the container was empty, he discarded it and went to the control console. He turned the ignition key and the craft's engine rumbled to life. He didn't shove the throttle forward right away. Instead, he reached into his pocket for the pack of matches Susan had given him. It was wet from his swim, but he hoped he could find at least one match that was dry enough to still light. He pulled a match free and ran its head across the striker without success. He tossed it aside and tried another. And another. And yet another. He was beginning to fear that the Mass was going to win simply because the goddamned matches had gone for a swim with him. But the sixth match sparked and caught fire. He was so surprised he nearly dropped it, but he held the flame to the rest of the matches to see if they would catch, too. At first they didn't, but then a few of the drier ones ignited. The flame they produced was feeble, but Jarrod thought it would be enough.

He tossed the entire pack aftward. It landed inside the hull and the gasoline Jarrod had splashed around ignited with a *whoosh*. It was the most satisfying sound he'd ever heard in his life. He eased the throttle forward and turned the steering wheel until the prow of the boat was pointed at the Mass. Once he had the boat aimed where he wanted it, he pushed the throttle the rest of the way forward and the boat raced forward, flames trailing behind it.

Jarrod felt a profound sense of peace settle on him. Whatever would happen next, he'd done his best to help Tasha combat the Mass, and that would have to be enough.

See you later, kiddo, he thought.

As the boat drew close to the Mass, he saw the battling sharks had moved closer to the edge. Only five of the initial eleven remained alive, but they were still going at each other as furiously as ever. Well, their fight would be over soon enough.

He'd lived a good life. He'd had an interesting career, had made many friends, and had enjoyed a modest amount of fame. Now he was going to go out on his own terms, giving his life to stop a real-life monster from claiming any more innocent lives. What more could a man ask for?

The boat was within ten feet of the Mass when Jarrod saw a shape emerge from the water on his left. The shark slammed into Jarrod, knocking him off the boat and into the water. He sank, arms and legs thrashing as he tried to stop himself from sinking.

He felt more than heard the sound of the boat colliding with the Mass. Orange light flared to life above him, and he knew his work was done. How much damage the Mass would take from the fire, he didn't know, but he'd done all he could. He stopped moving then and allowed himself to sink. He was tired, so very tired, and all he wanted to do was close his eyes and rest.

So he did.

CHAPTER FOURTEEN

Jarrod opened his eyes and saw the first rays of dawn on the water. He was lying on the beach, stiff and sore, but very much alive. He sat up, his body protesting, and he tried to remember what had –

And then it came back to him in a rush. The landsharks attacking Flotsam, the survivors fleeing to the roof of Susan's apartment building, Tasha being abducted by the Mass, Susan and him driving to the beach to rescue her, and everything that happened afterward. He remembered everyone who had lost their lives last night, with him – the man dying of leukemia – the sole survivor.

Irony's a bitch, he thought.

After a few moments he got to his feet and walked down to the edge of the water. He scanned the horizon but saw no sign of the Mass. He wondered if he and Tasha had managed to kill it or if it had survived and was still out there somewhere, licking its wounds and preparing to kill again someday.

He heard Tasha's thought-voice then.

"Hello, Jarrod. Don't bother replying. This is a message I implanted in your mind before I left. It's set to activate once you're awake enough to make sense of it. Here's what you missed.

Images flashed through his mind in rapid succession. The flaming bay boat colliding with the Mass, fire spreading across the creature's surface. He heard Inez's psychic scream of pain and anger as she tried to descend into the water to extinguish the flames, but Tasha prevented her from doing so. Inez fought to regain control of the Mass, and when all of her attention was focused on that effort, Tasha struck. She sent a bolt of psychic force into Inez's mind, and killed the woman as surely as if she'd slipped a knife into her heart. With Inez gone, it was a simple matter for Tasha to take control of the Mass, and she commanded it to go underwater and douse the flames. The fire had never been any real danger to the Mass; the creature was too large. But it had served to distract Inez, and in that sense had aided in her defeat.

While all of this had been happening, one of the Mass' Hunters – which Tasha had sent to keep Jarrod from sacrificing his life – took hold of his arm in its mouth, careful not to bite too hard, and carried him to shore. The Hunter, one of only a handful remaining to the Mass, returned to the ocean, and Jarrod was safe.

Tasha began "speaking" once more.

"The Mass' biology possesses incredible mutagenic abilities, and Inez was able to use them to transform the Hunters so they could survive out of the water. I hoped I might be able to use the Mass' power to cure your cancer, but I couldn't. The best I could do was use my psychic power to alter your brain so you will no longer experience any pain related to your cancer. You will still die, but your last days will not be miserable ones.

"The burn damage was relatively minimal, and it will heal soon. I'm the Mass now, and the Mass is me. It's kind of cool. I was a fan of horror movies, and now I get to actually be a monster. And I got to have an adventure alongside my favorite actor. No regrets there.

"I'm not sure what I'm going to do next. I'm low on Hunters, so I need to restock. Sharks are great, but I'm thinking of heading to Las Dagas *and snagging a few pliosaurs. I think they'd make kick-ass Hunters, don't you?*

"Don't worry; I won't hurt anyone. So long as the ocean's full of food, I won't need to. I'm glad you survived, and I hope you enjoy the time you have left. You've earned it. Goodbye, Jarrod."

"Goodbye, Tasha."

Jarrod turned and began walking up the beach. He didn't look back.

THE END

CHECK OUT OTHER GREAT DEEP SEA THRILLERS

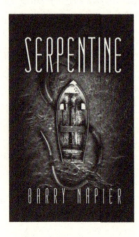

CHECK OUT OTHER GREAT
DEEP SEA THRILLERS

SEA RAPTOR
by John J. Rust

From terrorist hunter to monster hunter! Jack Rastun was a decorated U.S. Army Ranger, until an unfortunate incident forced him out of the service. He is soon hired by the Foundation for Undocumented Biological Investigation and given a new mission, to search for cryptids, creatures whose existence has not been proven by mainstream science. Teaming up with the daring and beautiful wildlife photographer Karen Thatcher, they must stop a sea monster's deadly rampage along the Jersey Shore. But that's not the only danger Rastun faces. A group of murderous animal smugglers also want the creature. Rastun must utilize every skill learned from years of fighting, otherwise, his first mission for the FUBI might very well be his last.

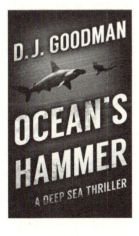

OCEAN'S HAMMER
by D.J. Goodman

Something strange is happening in the Sea of Cortez. Whales are beaching for no apparent reason and the local hammerhead shark population, previously believed to be fished to extinction, has suddenly reappeared. Marine biologists Maria Quintero and Kevin Hoyt have come to investigate with a television producer in tow, hoping to get footage that will land them a reality TV show. The plan is to have a stand-off against a notorious illegal shark-fishing captain and then go home.

Things are not going according to plan.

There is something new in the waters of the Sea of Cortez. Something smart. Something huge. Something that has its own plans for Quintero and Hoyt.

CHECK OUT OTHER GREAT DEEP SEA THRILLERS

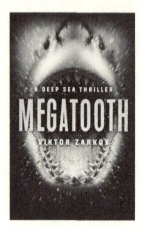

MEGATOOTH
by Viktor Zarkov

When the death rate of sperm whales rises dramatically, a well-respected environmental activist puts together a ragtag team to hit the high seas to investigate the matter. They suspect that the deaths are due to poachers and they are all driven by a need for justice.

Elsewhere, an experimental government vessel is enhancing deep sea mining equipment. They see one of these dead whales up close and personal...and are fairly certain that it wasn't poachers that killed it.

Both of these teams are about to discover that poachers are the least of their worries. There is something hunting the whales...

Something big
Something prehistoric.
Something terrifying.
MEGATOOTH!

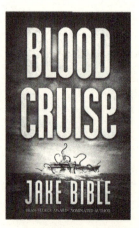

BLOOD CRUISE
by Jake Bible

Ben Clow's plans are set. Drop off kids, pick up girlfriend, head to the marina, and hop on best friend's cruiser for a weekend of fun at sea. But Ben's happy plans are about to be changed by a tentacled horror that lurks beneath the waves.

International crime lords! Deep cover black ops agents! A ravenous, bloodsucking monster! A storm of evil and danger conspire to turn Ben Clow's vacation from a fun ocean getaway into a nightmare of a Blood Cruise!

Made in the USA
Coppell, TX
21 May 2025

49649815R10090